Of FLINT *and* FORTUNE

CAMILLE DUPLESSIS

It's always for N.

AUTHOR'S NOTE

New 'round these parts, partner? You should read *The Kraken and the Canary* before *Of Flint and Fortune*. Paul and Alastair clamored for more attention even as I was trying to concentrate on Tom, Theo, David, and Lennie. Way back when I was finishing *Kraken,* I found the skeletons of *Of Flint and Fortune* and *Of Valentines and Visions* (out later this year), and they're companion stories.

Then they line up before *Like Silk Breathing, The Only Story,* and *Unfair Winds,* which I hope you've read or will read. If you have, you'll notice Benson and Mrs. Lloyd—with her unmarried surname—play their parts here! Benson is suspiciously, ambiguously in his upper middle age, and Mrs. Lloyd is a smidgeon older than Paul. This is the last story before The Queen Anne is renamed as The Shuck, too.

I seem to keep writing stories that work together like three-volume (or just serial) novels from the 1800s, which is either great or annoying depending on the day! In addition to these stalwart secondary characters, we also see more of Alastair's stepson, James, who is something of an unreliable narrator—in *Unfair Winds,* he implies he didn't hear much from his dad, but in reality, he ignores most of what his dad writes to him. (He even claims his mother is just out of the house when he overhears a certain salacious thing... that's not actually true.)

Also, on the subject of James and Alastair, I wanted to underscore a couple of social history factors that permeate Threads of Wyrd. First, sex between men wasn't decriminalized in England or Scotland until the latter half of the 20th century. (This can still impact how or if people come out.) There was, however, social acceptance within certain circles and contexts. Secondly, adulthood arrived quickly for Victorian folks. That doesn't mean everyone loved or condoned such harshness, of course.

1

EDINBURGH—OCTOBER, 1867

When Alastair Gow's periodic paramour moaned something to the effect of, "I'll give you everything" while in the throes of pleasure, he knew it was time to end things. Or ignore them. It shook him out of the moment, making him wonder if he'd completely misread the dynamics of their arrangement. Mostly, it underscored how he just wasn't enjoying himself as much as Mr. Albert Calder was.

Though he wasn't suffering and he hadn't been forced, the truth remained. One of them was *far* more enthusiastic than the other. Unfortunately, Bert was wealthy, repressed, and rather spoiled. He was a younger son, as well as one who preferred the company of other sons. Alastair still had the sense, though, that Bert generally received whatever he wanted out of people. Be it through charm, manipulation, or wheedling.

These were the weapons he had observed, and because he was desperate for intimacy, he tried to ignore them. Eventually, Bert wore Alastair down and cajoled him into sporadic fucking; he was tenacious as a bad cold. Even Lucas, the mate in common who'd introduced them about two years back, seemed to regret the introduction—and ordinarily, he passed remarks on how he enjoyed seeing Alastair inconvenienced.

Bert had lingered around Lucas since they were children, though only one of them had gone off to Cambridge and spent holidays in his family's hereditary country house in Norfolk. Idly, Alastair still wanted to know the story behind their acquaintance, yet had not bothered to ask. He rarely listened when Bert talked about that country house, much less their friend.

Whatever his reasons, Bert was fond of accompanying Lucas to pubs where he was as out of place as a hothouse orchid stuck in a snowdrift. Once he met Alastair, he only followed Lucas all the more readily to such places.

Almost patiently, Alastair waited for Bert to settle under him. But all the warm sensations of a moment ago had shifted from tolerably pleasurable to intolerably obtrusive. Nonetheless, he tried to be a gentleman, as much as a poor boy could grow up to be one.

Once Bert went still and wore a satisfied little smile on his face, Alastair got up, rising to his feet. Then he stood just opposite the bed. "That was lovely," he said. He couldn't blame Bert for looking rather stunned. If a lover got out of him and rose so quickly, he might be equally taken aback. "You need to go—James will be home soon."

Perhaps the last thing he wanted was his school-aged son walking in on such an assignation. There had been a small handful of ill-advised overnight stays, and each time, Alastair regretted both the risk of discovery and Bert's seeming predilection for sleepwalking and talking. This, however, was the afternoon, so at least one of those factors was not present.

"I..." Bert trailed off, the tendons in his neck working slightly as he swallowed.

"What? You can wash up." He nodded to the basin on a pretty little stand near the bed, where he'd left fresh water before Bert arrived.

The suggestion of James posing an interruption, no matter that there was in truth plenty of time before he returned, did seem to goad Bert into sitting up. His pale cheeks were flushed, and his blue eyes were bright in an unlined face framed by mussed, honey-colored hair.

Alastair had thought Bert was only infatuated. Even though he did not precisely enjoy playing the part of a coarser man for a rich one, he almost preferred it to declarations of *giving everything.* And Bert, unlike him, might end up blackmailed for what they did.

Nobody of note or high society could be that interested in Alastair. Besides, everybody said things they didn't mean in bed.

If Bert *was* serious, Alastair couldn't see how anything could grow between them. One was entitled to all the law would award him, whether or not that would happen, while the other had broken the law so many times. Of course, those days were essentially behind him; Bert must have suspected it due to where he resided and the quality of his possessions.

A slightly nervous flutter settled in his stomach. Ignoring the muffled chatter of a few women who passed outside the house, Alastair watched Bert wash perfunctorily, then dress himself. He made the familiar bedroom feel foreign, as though he should be there but Alastair should not. In truth, the furnishings were still too inexpensive for Bert, even if they weren't inexpensive at all.

Thanks to one good deed being repaid, Alastair could call this place home. He'd saved Miss Alice Adair from certain mistreatment and probable scandal some years ago. Her father had paid him handsomely; this had also ruined an impending housebreak he'd been planning with Lucas.

Because Alastair impulsively told Mr. Adair of the planned burglary when he'd brought Alice home, Adair had sold what they'd hoped to steal and furnished him with an inordinate reward, swearing Alastair to secrecy.

Lucas' mouth had gaped open at the formerly full room being empty of valuable curios and ancient jewelry, the likes of which had been taken from some rural cache and paid for by the Adair family.

Yes, Adair's gratefulness had changed things. These days, more for something to do, Alastair was sometimes a fence, a link between those who wished to move money or goods, and those who wished to procure said money or goods. It scratched a lingering itch for adventure. In reality, he didn't need to do it. He didn't advertise that change of status, for it would attract ire he didn't wish to deal with.

He still wasn't sure if Lucas knew of his involvement in the empty room at the Adairs' home. It was entirely possible that he did and merely waited to make it known. Such a thing wouldn't be unheard of in their world. Whatever the risks, Alastair was comfortable by his modest standards. He hadn't always been, and he hadn't thought he would be.

Whenever anyone had asked him what his plans for retirement were, he usually said dying early. He hadn't changed his answer, but it was now something of a lie.

"I hadn't quite recalled," said Bert, a little indulgently, "that your son would be coming home soon."

What he thought he was indulging, Alastair couldn't say. "I try to keep it in mind. He doesn't need to walk in on anything like this, and you don't need the embarrassment." He blinked the thought of his own financial status away, lest it be read in his eyes. Anyway, he was only thinking about it because it was impossible not to think about money when Bert was around.

His naked body bore signs of wealth, or at least a lack of much hardship. Not tanned, not too thin, not scarred, not pockmarked. When he was younger, Alastair might have been jealous. Today, he merely recognized a different experience from his. One might say a kinder one. In many ways it was, even though Bert still had an underlying air of neediness about him.

But Bert had never gone to bed hungry, his clothes and shoes had always fit him properly, and he'd never lacked anything material. Amidst all of that ease, Alastair was given to believe his father had been domineering and his mother had been frigid. They had the father in common. At least his own mother had been warm, telling him stories and giving him a hug whenever he needed one if she was not at work, or doing any of the household tasks his father refused to do.

Not all fathers are terrible. He was a middling one himself, and that was generous. Good fathers surely didn't think of leaving their sons. The first time he'd thought about leaving all of this behind, it was just a week since Evie passed. He hadn't; he was still here.

His thoughts were again drawn to Adair, a father who'd given quite a lot to an unknown man for bringing his daughter home safe. Without that boon, Alastair's home would be considerably less happy, from the cheerfully decorated bedroom to the kitchen and parlor tidied by a largely mute old woman who made the best bread he'd ever tasted.

But what he wouldn't give to be free as a bird, able to live as he wished.

He didn't blame James for his circumstances, which were due to some quirk of the universe that had left him pining for men with a romantic's heart, a waif's resources—until adulthood—and a father who had mocked the desire as soon as he noticed it. Alastair wondered, sometimes, if the early mocking he'd endured was why he settled for rather supercilious men like Bert whenever he wanted company.

The first time he brought Bert here, Bert seemed surprised he managed to have a charlady at all. He had brushed the dubious compliments away, making up a lie about being a widower whose late wife had been of modest means, but enough to leave him something.

He *was* a recent widower, but Evie's people hadn't had any money. The explanation didn't make much sense, but it held up if someone didn't poke at it. Luckily, the neighborhood itself was respectable, if not hugely prosperous.

"Of course," said Bert. As ever, he was polite. Alastair could never decide if he was almost oily rather than simply polite. After all, he'd been overly enthused about Morwenna, the bread-baking charlady. Then he did a decidedly more rude thing and glanced between Alastair's legs. "My boy, you weren't satisfied at all, were you?"

No, Bert couldn't love him. Nobody would look that way at any part of someone they loved, and they probably wouldn't address them with such a diminutive, either. Every time Bert did it, he cringed. He'd been called *boy* too many times, well into adulthood, by anybody who didn't want to afford him a modicum of respect. *Lad* was better, if dependent on who said it.

"That's all right. Being a father should take precedent." He did believe that, though he fell short at the endeavor. "And I just…" he glanced at the window, where the lavender curtains were drawn. He could still tell the sun was now lower. "I happened to notice the light changing outside."

Bert said, "I wager you'll see to yourself later."

Still unbothered by his own nudity, even though Bert was now fully dressed in his fine suit, Alastair said, "I might." He knew he was supposed to flirt.

As though Alastair had uttered something filthy, he said, "Naughty."

"You know me," said Alastair, rather at a loss.

Bert's eyes roved along his tattoos, following the line of his torso, then his legs. They provided a source of fascination for him, and Alastair didn't have the heart to point out tattoos were now something of a fad, even in good society. "Well," said Bert, "you shall have to describe it to me when next we meet."

Onanism had always held an appeal, so it wasn't the problem, but narrating his actions to Bert held very little interest. When Bert finally finished with his shoes, Alastair was dressed as well, though not in his own boots.

Bert stood again, rather shaky. "I'll see myself out, then."

Alastair hoped he wouldn't try for a kiss. He didn't mind it while they were in bed, but kisses away from that particular venue felt too intimate for him. He was quite interested in touch and companionship, which could win against common sense or feeling uncomfortable. "Yes," he said, waiting at the foot of the bed, one hand on the bedpost. Bert lingered so, and it made him want to fidget. "Morwenna isn't here, as you know, so... you'll be able to slip outside. James won't be rounding the corner yet."

Not that they would know one another even if they did cross paths.

Bert came close to him as he went to the door. "Thank you, darling."

Alastair wanted to say *for what*. "Of course."

When it must have become clear he was not going to get another kiss, Bert said, "À bientôt."

It wasn't until he had quit the room that Alastair allowed himself to think, *Pretentious fucker*.

HE CHANGED the bedlinens that night and felt guilty for going soft. In the past, depending on what he'd been doing, he might have had to tolerate sleeping in less than desirable circumstances. Another man's scent or worse on his sheets shouldn't bother him. Even if it always had, he'd believed he had to be hardened against having such preferences. If given his choice, he would have slept somewhere immaculate, always.

Although he'd rented this house for long enough that it did feel like his even if he knew it belonged to someone else, the looming fear that something—anything—would go wrong did sometimes surface. That he might lose his home was one such fear amongst many. His bed smelling different could dredge paranoia up from the depths of his mind, as weak as it felt to him to be swayed by such a small thing as scent.

He wouldn't say Bert ever smelled bad; he usually smelled of neroli. In light of what they'd done, the sheets smelled more sour than they did of any flowers, but Alastair had still slept in worse places. Dark corners in closes or pubs' rooms crawling with insects. A bit of someone's sweat should not have bothered him.

All the same, he'd been in bed for moments before he'd had to get up, root through the wardrobe for clean linens, and make the bed by the light of a single candle. He piled the dirty sheets on the floor, and no one would see them but him. James was past the age where he'd want to get in bed with his father, and he'd fallen asleep a few hours ago.

He was finally able to close his eyes and drift off, not to sleep, but somewhere moderately more peaceful. His heart wanted peace. It wanted safety, yet sometimes the best it could do was contain movement and dreams: rambling thoughts about warm lovers he would never meet, and of people who didn't believe the facade he had worked hard to build.

Maybe even someone who understood he wished so badly to help, to be a force of good, and wouldn't scoff because he'd spent years of his life raising another man's son. Or because he'd gone out of his way to rescue some girl from the machinations of the likes of him. He couldn't get too close to these traits in himself, though he kept them alive. They were as warm as a hearth fire that was a little too big.

Perhaps one day, he might meet someone who could

manage such closeness. As he tried to let himself fall asleep under the clean sheets and warm counterpane, all he firmly understood was Bert wasn't that sort of person.

2

CROMER—OCTOBER, 1872

Given Alastair had just that morning used a certain appendage in a manner considered illegal—but which brought them both immense pleasure—Paul found his evasiveness tiresome. There really could be no excuse for it once they'd engaged in many such activities together, and decided to live in the same flat as man and wife.

"You're just being obstinate," said Paul. He had asked about a letter Alastair secreted off, one of at least several lately.

"I'm not," said Alastair, "I'm just being private."

"It isn't a terribly invasive question. I see others' post." As a public house with rooms to let, they took letters and small parcels when customers couldn't be bothered to take them anywhere else.

"It's nobody."

"You're writing to nobody?" He had never seen the recipient's address, though he assumed Alastair paid for the postage.

Alastair crossed his arms over his chest and gave a sigh,

his body shifting under all his black clothes and settling again to stillness. "Paul."

Alastair knew *him* as intimately as possible, not only because of their physical relations, though those did feel as innate as gravity. Never had Paul divulged so much of his internal world to another. The lack of reciprocity was beginning to stifle the goodness Alastair brought into his life. Not entirely, but a little. The rogue knew about his first few visions. The first *tendre* he'd ever had—on his parents' butcher's son, who was all smiles and sparkling gray eyes. Then, as it happened, all soft lips and welcoming arms.

And Alastair knew about the time Paul's younger brother, Edward, pierced Paul's left ear with a filched sewing needle, a tiny gold hoop he'd found under a table in the taproom, and part of an apple for safety's sake. Mother and Father hadn't cared much about it, just as they hadn't minded Edward's long hair.

Yet Paul's experimentation with an earring ended the winter morning it caught on his scarf and nearly ripped his lobe.

Childhood fears, boyhood fancies, had all been given to Alastair, who was as steadfast a listener and supporter Paul could ask for. He adored Paul, and Paul knew it. That caused no disquiet. But by stark contrast, what Paul knew of his affectionate nightmare of a man was external, predicated on others in Alastair's life, and it rarely had anything to do with how *he* felt. He didn't know what kept him up at night, what had motivated him as a boy, and, least of all, who the letters were going to.

In the last thirteen months, Paul discovered Alastair's birthday was the twenty-third of July and there were twelve years between them depending on the time of year. He knew his mother was fond of folklore and ghost stories, but hadn't possessed preternatural abilities herself despite being dear friends with a local wise woman. He knew Alastair's father had hated seemingly everything, including Gaelic, cats, sweets, and his family's poverty.

He also knew, because he could sense strange auras that eddied around people if he concentrated, that Alastair was trying not to be so peeved. The pine green that often followed him shivered erratically before Paul blinked the vision away. Too distracting. He was glad it wasn't something that happened unbidden for him, as his premonitions did.

When they'd first met, Alastair revealed he'd once wished to have the chance at finding love, and that was possibly the most vulnerable thing he'd disclosed to date. It had brought them together in a roundabout way: at the time, Alastair was entangled in aiding Paul's childhood acquaintance, Miss Muriel Sykes, run away with her beloved Abigail.

The alternative of marrying a man whom she did not—and could not—love would've been bleak, even though Paul supposed he could have stepped forward as an alternative fiancé for her. If, of course, she could convince her father the change was an advantage, and he hadn't met Alastair just before discovering her sorry circumstances.

More to the point, she loved women and he loved men, so neither of them would've expected fidelity or love from the other.

Now her bastard of a father was cold in the ground; the circumstances of his death had been mysterious yet grimly appealing to most anyone who'd known him. It didn't matter; Muriel and Abigail were now safely residing in Scotland. Her two letters had said as much and given both Mr. Gow and Mr. Apollyon something of a standing invitation to pay them a visit near Edinburgh.

Rather touched, Paul didn't have the heart to tell her it was too difficult for business to take a holiday.

"You do write to someone. I just wondered who they are, is all. I don't even write to Edward much." He wanted to sound nonchalant as he reordered bottles on the shelf behind the bar. It was a quiet mid-morning. His brother must be busier than he was, particularly with a very young son toddling about underfoot. There had been fewer letters between them, of late, and he hadn't visited Norwich in ages.

In their childhoods, Edward would talk and he would listen. That was their natural order of things. It worked well, so Paul could understand someone who did not wish to speak overmuch. He was that way himself.

Still, Alastair chattered about everything but his innermost thoughts.

"Why would you?" Alastair said easily. "Norwich is close. You could see him as often as you wanted, or as often as you could stand to leave this place."

"So whoever it is, they're not nearby. Is it a relative?"

"Paul."

The canary that neither of them had the heart to cage all day chittered quietly from its perch on a nearby wooden chair, and Alastair's eyes rested upon its small flash of yellow rather than Paul. It did seem happy without Abigail or Muriel, its prior owners, but Paul assumed this was because it wasn't cooped up. If its freedom and happy demeanor meant cleaning up blessedly small piles of droppings in bizarre places, he didn't mind. He did, however, need to write and ask if the canary had a name.

He sighed. It was strange for Alastair, a man who would make remarks about this and that, to be so succinct. Just yesterday, he'd spoken for half an hour on the lore of a certain type of seer who could commune with the dead, all because he'd passed St Peter and St Paul after posting a certain letter, the very one instigating this conversation.

The seer's title was Gaelic, which Paul loved on Alastair's tongue. His mother had been fluent, but his father had discouraged her teaching him, so all Alastair could manage was to pronounce words properly. It sounded wonderful. Paul merely butchered it.

He suspected the lore about the seer had been meant to distract him.

Alastair did not seem to receive letters in return, not that Paul would necessarily know about any replies.

Whatever the secret was couldn't be so terrible. When one looked at Alastair, one couldn't conclude he was entirely respectable, but neither did he have an air of brutality. Paul thought it must be some kind of relation who was receiving the regular post, not a matter of bribery or worse. Without pausing to think of the consequences of what he was about to ask, for if he had, he might have heeded Alastair's cross expression, Paul said, "Why can't you just tell me?"

"It's none of your affair," said Alastair, leaning with both forearms on the bar, speaking with a new tinge of desperation.

Paul crossed his arms, noting the desperate tone and disliking its presence. He didn't doubt Alastair's heart or his intentions, but he did understand he'd need to tread lightly on the subject, or this would be the last he heard of it. Alastair was frightened, he realized. He tilted his head slightly, meeting deep brown eyes that had felt like a refuge since the day they'd met.

"It could be."

"You've got enough to be worrying about." Alastair waved a hand at the taproom. Empty now, but it would not be come nightfall. "I still marvel at how well you manage all this, and I'm only fucking helping, not doing nearly as much as you."

"It's not such a big place." Yet, despite only fucking helping, as he said, Alastair had become part of the place's fabric. If he was not present, people asked after him.

"It's insane."

"You wouldn't think so if it was all you'd ever done with yourself," said Paul, slipping him a smile, trying to imagine what exactly Alastair *had* done while growing up and failing in the specifics. "It's just making sure nothing falls through the cracks. And brewing things." He sighed, the smile sliding from his face. "Stop prevaricating."

"Angel, you know I won't," was the soft reply, quiet in its utterance but firm in its meaning.

Paul blinked and disregarded his need to make a retort. Alastair pushed back from the bar, standing up straight, and gazed at Paul warmly as though to soften the words. Then, with naught but a nearly apologetic smile, he quit the room.

The silence, thought Paul, was eloquent.

He knew Paul was desperate to know what was going on. Worse, Alastair wanted to be honest but found he still couldn't, his desire or good intentions to try, be damned. He didn't want to be known as a man who'd abandoned his son, or who'd accidentally double-crossed some of his associates, or who'd killed a handful of times. He'd never had the stomach for doing it out of enjoyment, and that he could at least say if pressed.

He had even thought about all of this during their first encounter, before they'd even kissed or done anything at all. Certainly, before he'd gone to Sykes' cottage simply to have a menacing word, and the drunk man had died tripping and hitting his head on a table.

Paul *was* younger than him, though he was not naïve, or intolerant, or even particularly disturbed by that accidental death. He had just asked, almost immediately, if anybody had seen Alastair entering or leaving the cottage. What held Alastair back from simply telling the whole truth now was fear of rejection. Fear of revulsion, more like. Where might he begin that wouldn't have Paul seeing him through new eyes that might no longer love him?

Alastair wasn't just someone who'd done nefarious things to survive. That category, he felt, Paul could digest.

No, you're also a bastard.

He was an adoptive father who'd married a woman to help himself and her, then left her son at the earliest opportunity that wouldn't leave the lad destitute. If sixteen was too young to be left on one's own, he wouldn't admit it. It wasn't cruelly done. He'd left because he felt cornered by life's turns, and rather like a sham besides.

At least Evie had possessed the good sense to take a good man, Arthur, as her lover. With Arthur's blessing, the child of their affair was legally Alastair's, sharing his surname. Their neighbors knew the truth of it. He and Evie were not the first people to have such an arrangement. Not when divorce was a costly process, if even possible, and separation wasn't particularly desirable. So the situation wasn't openly criticized or derided, but it was very likely discussed over pints and out of his hearing.

If James's continued silence in reply to his circumspect letters and sums of money, including the rent and payment of the charwoman who'd been with them since James was little, were any indication, there was a grudge.

He couldn't blame him. *But when I was his age, I...*

Stole and scrapped as one of the younger members of a gaggle who, had it been the Edinburgh of decades earlier, might've been aligned with resurrection men or other such covert characters. There was the occasional matter of killing, but it could not be said any of them made it a daily habit.

The creak in the floor under his feet brought him back to Cromer. He nodded to one of the newer maids as they passed each other near the bottom of the stairs. Molly was a quiet creature, though he could tell from her expressive brown eyes that he intimidated her. Part of it was out of his control, for his looks did tend to have that effect. And he had too many visible tattoos for them to be considered fashionable.

Though there was something of a fad on, they still needed to be largely hidden or quite small not to cause much of a stir. Most people he encountered within respectable society gave them a second glance. So he leaned into his most gregarious tendencies to hide the sense that he felt he didn't belong among upstanding people. It worked: he could win almost anybody over if given a few spare moments.

Paul never cringed or scoffed at them. Instead, he ran his

fingers along the ink as though he traced an engraving interwoven among precious stones on a ring. Still, Alastair suspected that even his incredibly empathetic seer might draw the line at abandoning a child. Paul had not yet looked at him as though he were lesser than, but Alastair had purposely given him little to evaluate. Although he was older, he felt far less wise. He didn't want to find out if he could bear Paul's censure.

Pushing guilt to one side, Alastair told himself James had Arthur, his blood father and a friend of his parents. He had work in Arthur's bakery, and a house, and everything he might need.

Save his adoptive father, who had tried to be loving and ultimately failed at the attempt.

When he went outside to the street and turned to the sea, he knew Paul was likely watching from a window, silently wondering what he'd done wrong. *Not a blessed thing.* The breeze chilled his face and he turned his overcoat's collar up, hunching his shoulders as he walked. He longed for warmth, but a cold walk served his mood much better than The Queen Anne's feelings of home and comfort.

"Mr. Gow." He ignored the hoarse voice. "Mr. Gow, don't ignore me when you're well aware I'm your beau's favorite."

He sighed, turned, and eyed Benson, a cantankerous fellow with immortal looks, which was only to say there was no definitive way to ascertain how old he was. He appeared to be in his middle age, but Alastair would posit nothing more specific than that. His clothing, all in various shades of muddy brown, was dated: Alastair's pickpocketing-practiced eye only told him Benson probably did not have anything on his person worth stealing.

"Benson." He was only Benson; if there was a given name attached to it, Alastair didn't know. It might've been his given name. There was also no Mr. appended to Benson. Perhaps to nobody's surprise, for they both were outsiders in their fashion, they got on like a house aflame since being introduced. A very inebriated Benson had declared if Alastair hadn't been Paul's, he might have tried his hand at capturing Alastair's interest.

Isn't it a pity I prefer women? he'd said to Paul, whose reddening ears were the only indication of his embarrassment.

Alastair had laughed, feeling safe enough in the busy taproom to laugh instead of disavow. Then Paul had explained, while the pink in his ears and the tip of his nose subsided, Benson was a friend, and he always spoke nonsense. The latter wasn't entirely true. Benson was prone to speaking in a manner that Alastair's mother would've called kenning, and he rarely deviated from truths. One just had to be sure they untangled Benson's meaning properly. If he said Alastair was Paul's, that was that.

Later during the same evening, in the dark of their bedroom and in a quiet punctuated by muffled snores from somewhere within the building, and the cries of gulls on the beach against the surf, Paul told Alastair he hadn't yet spoken to Benson about their new situation. But he was uncanny, so if he knew, it wasn't strange.

A witch? suggested Alastair.

Paul confirmed it. *Witch-hunter,* he'd said. *His family trade.*

"This is no day for a walk."

"It is," said Alastair. He still had no notion of what a witch-hunter was, but that Benson had magic wasn't in question. For Alastair, who had none at all, the effect of being near Benson was rather similar to the air during a storm. Benson's presence sometimes made the hairs on the backs of his arms stand up, not out of any fear, but more as a quality of being nearby. Since he enjoyed the new and strange, it didn't bother him.

Benson's manner of dress was rather similar to a wizard's, though, no matter what any ordinary person might try to dismiss. At first glance, he appeared to be all old clothes and careless layers. But on several occasions, Alastair had seen delicate silver or pewter charms woven into his shoulder length, ash-colored hair, as well as his unkept beard. He sported several such today, all glinting in the weak autumn sun.

"If you like being half-frozen," Benson said.

"You'd best go get warmed up, then." He'd probably been on his way to The Queen Anne when he'd seen Alastair walk outside.

"I'm sure your Mr. Apollyon will have something to my taste."

"He always does."

"Once you've made your way back, seek me out. Looks like there's a lot on your mind, so I shan't interrupt you now."

Settling his old bowler hat, one he'd found on a bench in a park one afternoon, against a gust of wind, Alastair asked, "Why?"

"Got a little message for you from a lass called Evie. It doesn't make much sense to me, but she said you had been married, so..."

3

———

It stopped him dead. He knew this was what Benson wanted him to do, judging by his expression of self-satisfaction, and it irked him. Despite what he'd said mere moments earlier, Benson *wished* to interrupt him. But Alastair wasn't irked enough to do something else and defy his expectations. He sighed and straightened his shoulders, too aware of Benson's peculiarities to question what or how he knew about Evie.

Coincidence might be to blame, but there still remained the fact that Evie had been dead for over five years. He'd never breathed a word about her to anyone in Cromer, Benson included. He was unashamed of having been married, but the weight of making the revelation felt too heavy for him to gather the courage to do it. "We can't talk about *that* in The Queen Anne."

"You mean, you can't talk about it near Paul. Doesn't he know you had a wife by now?"

Resigned, opening his mouth and finding it difficult to

speak, Alastair said, "No." Silly of him to be thinking of coincidence.

"These things have a way of coming out, you know."

"I know. But in truth," said Alastair, peering over Benson's shoulder in the direction from where he'd come, and where Benson had been heading, "I expected I would be dead before I ever fell in love, and before my widowed state might matter to somebody." The street wasn't deserted, but neither was Paul anywhere to be seen. He didn't quite expect he would be out of doors so soon, but felt luck wasn't quite on his side today.

"That's no way to live a life, is it? Not for a great romantic."

"As I just said, I didn't think I'd be alive this long." It was rather grim, but he reckoned he'd be dead by some twist of circumstance, perhaps quite a normal and predictable one. Dead by someone whom he'd crossed or slighted, by some drunken mishap—he'd never had much to drink or taken drugs while working, but anyone could make a careless mistake—or by illness.

No one in his world seemed to live a long, happy life, and this had instilled some amount of hedonism within him. The sort that told him enjoyment was worth it because tomorrow wasn't promised. Meanwhile, being realistic about what fate might have in store for his ultimate end was crucial, so he would not call himself too foolhardy.

He didn't live with any particular trepidation about dying, but he also hadn't considered he'd meet someone like Paul. Now that he had, and it was clear how much Paul did matter, he was rather at a loss. Love this profound was a radical change to his self-knowledge. He hadn't fully acclimated to it.

"I'm glad you *are* with us," said Benson.

Meeting Benson's eyes, Alastair said, "We can go to The Bell, seeing as you don't want to catch a chill." He offered a tiny smile, for he couldn't really be angry. It wasn't Benson's fault he could clearly see beyond what most could. Since he was not given to any orthodoxy, it didn't unnerve him the way it might bother a religious man.

Again he thought of Paul, of all the things he could see and did see, and the way he delivered such impossible knowledge with an air of somebody remarking upon the weather. Just last week, he'd cautioned a woman visiting her relatives in Cromer against walking along the promenade in her new chartreuse hat, though he hadn't specified why to anybody but Alastair, who was privy to the information that a gull was going to ruin it.

When the woman came back to The Queen Anne that afternoon, it was with bird shit spattered along the hat. Some might think of coincidence there, too, but Alastair knew Paul's well went deeper than coincidence could. No amount of assuring her the hat could be cleaned, or that some people felt such a misfortune was actually good luck, consoled the woman.

"The Bell, hey?" Benson shrugged. "I much prefer your lover's public house, but as far as others go, it's certainly not the worst."

It was, in Alastair's opinion and vast experience of public houses, passable. The Bell was coarser than anyone in the Apollyon family would ever allow their establishment to become, but not unsafe or unwelcoming. Just less strict with its intoxicated clientele, more openly accommodating of other vices, and it was rundown in comparison to The Queen

Anne. It did not generally offer its few upstairs rooms to customers, either.

Muriel had used one to secret Abigail away upon her arrival to Cromer and before they left. Alastair wondered what she'd told her employer, and why she hadn't used The Queen Anne. At the time, she'd been working as a barmaid at The Bell. He suspected she might have lied and said they were looking for male customers. In which case, Alastair could imagine the landlord allowing the arrangement for a brief moment. In exchange for a later fee, of course.

He led the way to The Bell through active streets, busy even past summer, itching to know what message Benson might have had for him. He stopped neither to make polite chatter with his companion nor to greet the few acquaintances he saw on the way. Benson didn't seem to care for polite anything, and none of the acquaintances Alastair had made while residing in Cromer were the sort who really had moments to spare.

It wasn't until they'd entered the pub, Alastair bought the pints, and they'd settled in the smokiest alcove that Benson resumed their conversation. "Mind you, I don't *enjoy* talking to the dead. They just don't respect me, sometimes, and I don't get a choice in the matter at all."

Alastair must have looked more confused than he wanted to, for Benson added, "Oh, yes, I know she's dead."

That wasn't what confused him. He chuckled. While he'd probably ask sometime precisely how Benson could talk to ghosts, he was not as interested in logistics at present. "If you think I can't believe that you talk to ghosts, you'd be wrong. Think of who I live with. Think of what he does. All those visions. You blathering to a specter isn't what gives me pause." Alastair didn't want Benson to think they had gossiped about him, so he didn't mention any witch talk. "And you look like a Druid."

If he wasn't mistaken, Benson looked pleased in the diffuse smoke. "Well…"

Alastair sipped his beer; it wasn't nearly as good as anything Paul brewed. He had not recalled The Bell's being so lackluster, but when he'd frequented the place over a year ago, he and Paul hadn't yet met. "It's more, I can't see how Evie would be disrespectful." She'd been more than a match for him and his boisterousness, but she wasn't anything he'd term as disrespectful. Bright and convicted, but not pushy or crude. He missed her.

"Might not be the best word for her," said Benson. "Adamant."

"That sounds more like it."

"She said you need to be careful."

"I'm never careful."

"She said that, too."

"How?" Alastair sat back in his chair, one of the spindly, wooden variety that he could never be sure would hold his weight. While The Queen Anne was also an old building with at least a century to her name, The Bell was either older or in worse repair. Its furniture was no different from its walls, and if it wasn't older than what Paul kept in his own pub, it was generally cheaper and less taken care of.

Many of the times Alastair had been here, he'd been pleasantly almost-drunk at the end of a day, which was when he could let his guard down and trundle to his rented rooms not so far away. He hadn't given much thought to the safety of chairs. In this moment, he was almost convinced he'd end up on the floor with one wrong stretch. Benson, slighter and less sturdy than him, appeared untroubled.

"How did I see her, you mean? Well, I'll tell you, it was a ghastly thing for her to do, appearing in a mirror the way she did. I almost slit my own throat shaving." He scoffed and said, "I've only the one mirror, and now it's covered."

Frowning, Alastair said, "She wasn't a witch."

"What a lovely thing that'd be—there would be fewer ghosts," said Benson, after a long gulp, leaving Alastair to consider how many ghosts the man had met. "No, you don't have to have a bit of witchery to your name to end up a ghost."

"Oh." He considered it, and found the immediate problem to be of more interest than anything so deeply philosophical. "Wait, how the hell is she haunting you? I doubt she'd try to haunt me. I wouldn't notice, mate. I'm not connected to anything like that." He had a great many talents depending on one's definition of the word. But any kind of preternatural awareness was beyond him. He accepted its existence and loved the stories, and that wasn't the same thing.

"She's not." Benson held up a lined palm as though to stay him. "She's not haunting anybody. Gone, she is, after she said her bit. It's like that, sometimes. God or the universe decides to throw something in your direction, so someone who loves you decides to speak up."

This was too theoretical. "Something's coming? Why not try to say it to me, then?"

"Would you listen, even if she could get through? Regardless, you were just saying you wouldn't notice."

"Fair point."

"It's about Adair's money, whatever the fuck that is," said Benson. "I couldn't understand much." Alastair nearly felt the words like a punch, but he let Benson continue without comment. "Something about it, or people around it—she said not to lie when somebody, a Lucas, comes to pay a visit and bother you."

Feeling the barest ire as the punch's shock subsided, Alastair said, "But you can't be more specific than that?"

"She was using my only mirror to talk to me. It's not perfect," said Benson tartly. "She showed up, she said she was your wife and told me you had an adopted son named James. *Then* she was on about Adair, and money, and someone called Lucas. It was like speaking into a well, all echoey and hollow."

Silent, because none of that was anything he could contest, Alastair drank more of his pint. Heedless of the taste, he waited for the alcohol to warm him briefly. Then, he muttered, "Anything else?"

"Whoever's bothering about this shit, and I would guess it's that Lucas person... she said he asked your son where to find you. Well, not your son, so much as his father. Your son blurted it out."

"Fuck."

"Your Evie, she said James and his father... they're all right."

"She was never mine."

After a few more moments of pensive silence passed, Benson added, "I can't be asking my brother, who shares his house with me, to tolerate dark stuff like the dead, so it had to be a quick exchange." Benson guzzled more beer. "Anyway, it wasn't a strong connection. She was nothing to me, after all, and her only link to me is you. Haven't known you so long, have I?"

Apparently, it didn't matter. Benson had enough of a story to make up for any lack of time. The vague idea of asking Paul if Benson might let a room from them crossed Alastair's mind, but he was too occupied by the collision of past and present that had presented itself in the weird man before him.

Had he been less inundated by half-formed thoughts and objections, the overwhelming sensation of *Shit, what on earth do I do now* clawing to the forefront of his mind, he might have admitted the uncanniness could merely follow Benson from place to place. If the specter of a strange woman could get through to him at his brother's house, she could surely do so under The Queen Anne's roof.

FEW THINGS WERE as annoying as a vision that happened in the middle of working. Paul likened them to headaches or sometimes small splinters, explaining to Alastair that they might be rather incapacitating, as a headache could be. At other times, the premonitions could be irksome, like a little splinter.

At present, this one was the terrible headache type. It was a shame; the taproom was full. Eight in the evening meant it usually was. With a small shudder, Paul steadied himself with a hand on the cool, whitewashed wall. He didn't recognize either of the two men he saw, and could see more clearly when he closed his eyes. Pink-cheeked fellows, maybe because of warmth Paul couldn't feel, each in an apron dusted in varying degrees of flour.

They seemed close, unless he missed his guess; one was older and the other was a young man of perhaps seventeen. While the older one appeared more jovial, his companion had a sullen air. As Paul concentrated, their muffled conversation became just clear enough for him to understand what they said. Wafts of baking bread were stronger to his nose than their words were to his ears, yet he could make it out as though he were eavesdropping on someone's conversation in a far corner while he stood across the room.

"You might consider replying," the older one said. He felt quite benevolent, like he'd be calm in any dire situation.

"Why?" The young man was visibly agitated. "He left, and now he thinks he can bribe me?"

"It isn't a bribe. He cares about you. He even kept Morwenna on." The elder one seemed infinitely patient, thought Paul, so he concentrated on him and let that serve as a tether to the vision. Thank goodness for small blessings; he was in the corridor just off the taproom, the one that featured the door to the cellar. If he looked as though he was having a turn, as he likely did—although he'd never thought to ask anyone what he looked like while he had a waking vision— he hoped nobody would discover him until things concluded.

He kept his palm flat on the wall and continued to focus on the calm, older man. These men spoke with an accent similar to Alastair's, but the room and their surroundings were hazy. Whether or not the haziness was because of the time of day wherever or whenever they were, he couldn't tell the precise location. A kitchen, perhaps, or a bakery, given all the flour and the enticing scent of bread.

"He never cared about me." The young man's lip jutted slightly, as though he were about to cry and fought the urge. "He cared about Mother, maybe."

"He loved her, in his way. He always cared for you, too." A pause as the elder man wiped his hands of flour, brushing them on his apron. "I don't expect you to understand, but it was for the best. Or at least, we all thought so." Gently, he added, "I'm sorry. It was a strange arrangement. Now, I don't think we should have carried on quite as we did."

This merited an almost-smile from the lad. "I wish you'd met her before they had ever married."

"I'm glad to have met her when I did. I always considered him a friend. Try to see it from his perspective... he must have felt trapped."

Whose perspective? Paul frowned out of confusion and continued concentration.

"Seems like he never thought anything through. He's even told me in a letter. Can you believe telling me something like *that* in a letter? Not that I haven't been able to guess by now."

"James..." the older one sounded quite tolerant of the younger one's mulishness. "Just reply to Alastair. He wouldn't be sending you money if he didn't care for you."

Paul had rarely felt his heart drop to his stomach. It was an unfamiliar sensation, despite having been a child of skittish disposition. This wasn't fear or nerves, though; it was sharp disappointment as he thought of Alastair's mysterious letters and understood that this young, frustrated man was their recipient.

So Alastair was, what, his stepfather? He was evidently helping with James' upkeep. Paul did not have any issue with that and in fact, if he were less stunned, he would approve. He did not wonder why the money was not going to The Queen Anne or to him. He didn't need it. But there was very little room for any approval at present; he was too consumed by shock.

Then he thought about how perceptive it was to say Alastair must have felt trapped, for what man whose love tended toward the supposedly deviant wouldn't feel caught in this situation?

Some who were more docile, perhaps, or more placid, might not. But neither docile nor placid were words he would use to describe Alastair.

He attempted to stop his mind from running away, and focused instead on what he still witnessed. The two people before him did not seem so very alike, but now that he knew to look for it, he saw shared little gestures, the smallest of tells that they were related.

James turned away. "That money is bribes. That's all. He knows he's behaved like a—" Paul heard the sneer in his voice and winced with his eyes still shut. "Bastard. Stealing away without a word. Naught but a note."

"If it's just bribes, give it back." That was said with the faintest of amusement. "And stop ignoring most of what he writes."

"I'm not stupid. If all that man is going to give me is his name and some money, then the money is of far more use. I'm not above being bribed."

Again, the older man sighed, this time more heavily, all traces of levity gone from his countenance. The gesture seemed to rile James, who turned back with the sneer that had been in his voice now plainly writ on his young face.

"You're little better. What kind of man lets another man raise his son?"

"Paul?"

It wasn't coming from the vision. Almost the same accent as the flour-dusted men's, but it was deeply grounded in Paul's own realities.

Caught between these new revelations and a confluence of different moments, it took him several moments to open his eyes. He looked up at Alastair in the corridor's semidarkness. He found he wanted to cling to him while demanding clarification. Instead, he still lingered near the wall.

"You all right, angel?" Alastair had been privy to enough premonitions to know that touching Paul immediately after he'd come out of one might result in a startle. He kept his distance, although Paul wagered Alastair wanted to reach out and pet him.

In response to that question, Paul decided to lie. "Yes, just..."

"That was an intense one, by the look of it," said Alastair, his eyes impossibly warm in the faint light.

"Very."

"Well, I wanted to say, Miss Garland is minding Maeve. She was doing that thing where the wee sparks come from her left pointer finger—you know how it happens after Maeve has a couple of pints of bitter—so Miss Garland brought her away from the curtains."

Faintly, Paul found the strength to smile, hoping he didn't look like he was puzzling over anything. "She's lovely."

Alastair meant Clemence, a close friend of several years who'd taught Paul all manner of cures for hangovers. For some semblance of public propriety and so they would not slip up around customers, they both generally referred to her as Miss Garland.

According to her, it made sense for a landlord to know these cures, and Paul agreed. Some, his father had known and handed down, while others were new to his repertoire.

She also often told him of the latest naughty act she'd read about in books of dubious legality that had been published in Paris or Amsterdam, and somehow secreted into England. Paul's father likely knew very little about *them*. They weren't old tisanes for sore heads and roiling stomachs. She used the acts on her clients. Paul used them on Alastair.

Though, the first thing of Miss Garland's he had used on Alastair was one of her concoctions for too much drink. But it wasn't long before he was able to use one of the acts to great effect. As he quickly discovered the first morning after, he was less skilled at laundering linens than he was at getting them dirty. Thankfully, he was able to send them to the laundress Miss Garland herself used to avoid incriminating questions.

Because she was also a courtesan like Miss Garland, she was undaunted by the sort of stains resulting from experiments inspired by Parisian-published play. All the rest of The Queen Anne's various sheets and cloth went to the usual person, the same his parents had employed; his and Alastair's often went to Miss Garland's loyal laundress.

Though it was usually a source of amusement, when Paul thought about all this just now, he found he had the greatest urge to sit down.

Everything had felt much better when he hadn't possessed so *many* unanswered questions.

"Are you *sure* you're all right? I'll mind things if you want to go up and rest," said Alastair, searching his face.

"I don't need to rest." *I need you to let me in.* Perhaps Miss Garland had some new maneuver that might help him coerce answers out of a recalcitrant, gorgeous man.

"If you say so. Hard to see in here, but you seem pale." Paul didn't doubt it. He felt too much to believe he looked unshaken. "It's full, but everybody seems well behaved tonight. I don't know if they need both of us, especially with Miss Garland there. It's almost like she works here—exemplary customer."

Despite wanting to focus on what he'd just been shown, Paul thought of how pleased he was with the progress Alastair had made in being a landlord's second-in-command. Almost everyone started when they were much younger than a man in his thirties. It had been with a bit of skepticism that he allowed Alastair to take up the work, figuring if he wasn't suited, he didn't have to keep at it. Perhaps to both their surprise, he was.

Shaking his head slightly, Paul said, "Exemplary friend." Whatever he had just seen was only a sliver of what was, and he reckoned it would happen very soon judging by the men's manner of dress.

He could draw at least one conclusion no matter what transpired: Alastair was indeed hiding rather large parts of himself. Never having cared before when it came to a lover, and being a great advocate for privacy, Paul wasn't prepared for how much he cared. He needed to know about the man he had been sharing his life with. Not because he was afraid of what Alastair might do, or of what he had done.

It wasn't difficult to surmise Alastair had done dark deeds, but he was not the sum of those. While it might sound childish if voiced aloud, Paul believed his beloved was quite a gentle person, even if his life had demanded a certain harshness from him. He wanted to savor Alastair like a favorite book that he had reread many times. But Paul got the sense Alastair felt any attempt to know him was akin to an attack on his autonomy. That such attempts were judgement or evaluation, not loving curiosity.

"She's lovely, as you said," Alastair said agreeably. On a soft breath, he reached out and rested careful fingertips on Paul's left shoulder, stroking him as one would a cat. The touch allayed any desire Paul had to ask questions, pulling him from his questioning mind to his willing body.

For now, that feeling was the lure he'd allow to catch him.

"Come on," Paul said, thinking rather fondly of all the regular customers who knew he and Alastair were together, yet never managed to say anything about it in all their incessant conversations about this and that, "let's reappear, or we shall never hear the end of it from anybody, especially Miss Garland."

4

———

He figured if he was sharing a bed with a seer who could divine things in his sleep, this wouldn't be the last time he woke with blood trickling from his nose. It was a wonder it hadn't happened before now. Alastair sat up slowly with a grumble, letting his eyes adjust, and brought a hand to his face. Satisfied his nose wasn't actually broken, something he'd experienced more times than he cared to count, he trailed his fingers the short distance underneath to his upper lip and felt tacky wetness.

Sniffing, he glanced down at Paul, who wasn't thrashing at this present moment.

He never really knew if he was supposed to wake him, or if, as with a sleepwalker, he was supposed to let him be. It was not his first experience with such things, whether natural or preternatural, though he did not suffer from them himself. Thanks to Bert, who had never lived with him but *had* managed to say and do strange things in his sleep each time they spent a night together, Alastair was vaguely familiar with the act.

Whatever Paul experienced seemed worse. He often had visions in his sleep, not every night, yet often enough. It was an interesting presentation of symptoms, for they did seem distinct from dreams, even to an outsider.

Paul looked as though he was in the deepest throes of concentration whenever they happened. He corroborated this was the case when he awoke, and his facial expressions were remarkably normal, only his eyes were closed. Alastair, who made a great study of Paul at all times, was intimately aware of how he looked in a multitude of situations.

When the thrashing started again, Alastair allowed him about a minute before he decided to try to wake him. Paul was struggling, almost like he was swimming or trying to swim. Or maybe he was bound up, wherever he was in his mind's eye. As Alastair regarded him, he noted Paul's hands were pressed together despite his wriggling.

Perhaps just a nightmare, then? Everyone had them.

Still, he wasn't sure. This felt too emblematic of what he'd seen before Paul confirmed he'd been having a vision, and they did seem to come in gaggles. He'd already had one earlier.

Wincing a little, because Alastair didn't quite know what reaction this would produce, he used his clean right hand to take Paul's left one. He gently entwined their fingers and pulled it slowly toward his own chest. With a great gasp, Paul wrenched his eyes open and they were only unfocused for a moment before landing upon Alastair. He knew he must be outlined against the moonlight.

Fortunately, Paul neither lashed out, nor made a sound past the gasp.

Smiling, Alastair whispered, "You bloodied my nose."

"God, did I?" Paul's voice was just as quiet, though hoarser than his own.

"You did."

"I... sorry."

Rather than relinquish his hand, Alastair squeezed it lightly. "It's all right. I got to wake up to you, so it's not so bad. I might get up and wash my face, though. Blood is itchy when it starts to dry."

Nodding once, Paul said, "Just give me a moment. The thought of candlelight is a bit much."

"Don't think I need it," said Alastair, "look at what the moon's giving us." He tilted his chin to indicate the window behind him, but didn't take his eyes from Paul.

"Clouds never manage to move properly during daylight, do they?"

"Eh, but this is beautiful." Alastair didn't mean the light or the bedroom, and he could tell Paul blushed even in just the gray tones the moon afforded them. Carefully, he bent forward and pressed a kiss to Paul's lips, mindful of his own nose. As Paul reciprocated with verve, he chuckled a bit and drew away. "I'm not keen on the taste of my own blood."

"Do you... like the taste of other people's blood?"

"Fair question," Alastair said, "but no." *Maybe we should just go back to kissing.* He pushed back the covers and stood, the wooden floor cool under his bare feet. Though he didn't mean to peacock, he had some hope that his nudity would put Paul into a better disposition. It often did. As he went to the basin, discovering there was indeed enough illumination, he asked, "Do you want to talk about it?"

"Talk about what?"

"Well, I'm not sure if it was a vision, or a dream." He felt

Paul's indecision keenly, as though it were a housecat ready to chase him across the room because he had dangled a string before it.

"It wasn't a dream," Paul said.

Splashing a bit of water onto his face, Alastair counted to five before replying. He didn't wish to spook Paul by pressing him, and there had been marked tension of late around divulgences. He knew all of it was his fault. Nonetheless, he wasn't ready to change course or apologize. "It seemed bad, whatever it was."

Though he wanted to know more, he waited. Massaged the spare amount of blood from under his nose and his nostrils. Flicked more water against his skin because it was bracing. His hair got some of it, but that couldn't be helped unless he tied it back. He didn't have anything to hand for the task, so he resigned himself to a few damp strands around his forehead.

"It was awful," said Paul, when enough moments had passed for Alastair to think he wasn't going to say anything, or he'd fallen back asleep despite everything. And he sounded so tiny, small enough that Alastair wanted to rush back to him. "I've never had one so perilous."

Instead of rushing, he looked for something to dry his face and did so, taking his time. He could be an anchor for his seer, even if he couldn't yet let him in. He'd stay calm; he'd steady him. "What happened?" With the words, he turned to the bed and went to resettle himself.

"I..." When Paul paused and shook his head, Alastair thought he might not say after all. "Is it silly to say I don't know?"

"No." Alastair made sure he was near enough to Paul for

him to touch him if he wanted to, but tried not to crowd him. The bed wasn't enormous, yet it was still big enough for both of them to have a bit of room. "Not at all. Your mind is a marvel, so it's not for me to call it silly." He smirked a little. "Well, if it's all your mind. Might be your soul. No idea how you do what you do."

"Nor me." Paul's smile was shaky. "I don't know what happened. But I was me. In my own body." He flinched, the smile slipping from his face. As Paul's smile disappeared, so too did Alastair's smirk. "In deep water, and I couldn't swim back to the surface. I think I was tied up? At the…" he rubbed idly at his wrists. "At the wrists. Maybe the ankles, too. I didn't think to look down, but it felt like I was."

"Jesus."

"I know it's getting cold at night. But it wasn't that." Paul swallowed, the discomfort and fear plain in his eyes. "I've never been that cold." Even if he was having some reservations, he still groped for Alastair's hand. Without hesitation, Alastair took his, shifting so that their bodies touched thigh to thigh. Paul wore a thin nightshirt, but in all his moving from the moments before, it had bunched around his stomach.

"No other context. Nobody tying me up and throwing me in," Paul said.

"That wouldn't make it any less terrifying."

"No, but if someone's planning to, it might be useful to have seen their face."

His pronouncement gave Alastair some pause. "Have you ever seen yourself in peril, like this?"

After a long exhale, Paul said, "I haven't. Funny, isn't it? That sort of thing is in all the stories, yet I've never been prone to seeing dire shit. Not happening to me, anyway." He trailed off, then spoke again. "Not really for anybody else, actually. Certainly not being tied up and drowned."

"We've talked about it a little," said Alastair, as everything in his body rebelled against the thought he was about to voice, "but if you've seen it, does that mean it *has* to happen? I thought not."

He felt Paul's leg tremble against his. He so rarely saw Paul shaken, much less scared. Without thinking about whether he would dislike it, Alastair embraced him so that his own back was against the headboard and Paul was against his chest.

"I don't think it means it *has* to happen. I've seen multiple versions of things in visions, before. It was only after something had passed that I knew, though." Paul sighed. "I've never felt myself in that kind of danger." He nestled himself closer, still trembling a little, and Alastair tried to breathe evenly.

Something else was occurring to him, and he couldn't ignore it for all he wished to remain steadfast and serene. It was Benson's message from Evie that had him in such a frame of mind, and it didn't seem like a trivial thing for Paul to suddenly see himself in peril after years of *not* seeing it.

He'd removed the blood from his face to prevent an itch, but now he felt a great internal itch. Paul had never seen anything so dire, as he said.

Does that mean I brought it to him?

He didn't want to believe he had, or that he'd brought danger to Paul's door, however far ahead it could be. "Well, I'll die before I let someone do anything of the kind to you."

He meant it. He might not be able to explain himself or

justify choices he'd made as a younger man. But he knew he'd have to be dead before anyone could place Paul Apollyon in such dark depths.

Softly, Paul said, "I know." It sounded to Alastair like there were other thoughts locked behind it, but none came to the fore.

With a relieved sigh, he kissed the top of his head and tried to put his mind to things that would matter come morning. An impending grocery delivery, an appointment with a prospective new cook because the present one was expecting a child and having trouble with the smell of food. He loved that Paul wasn't just going to dismiss her; the plan was to let her work as a maid until such a time when she could cook again. Having had a maid's position at the Langham before she came to Cromer, it was well within her scope.

Keeping his thoughts to mundane little things was much more pleasant than wondering if he'd brought misfortune to their circumstances. If, somehow, when he'd quickly and innocently decided to rescue Alice Adair from a ruffian and return her to her father, he had enraged Lucas enough to cause trouble now. The notion did play into his tendency to believe he did not deserve any goodness. If he wasn't careful, with all its familiarity, believing he was at fault might be more seductive than preserving the life he had built.

MORNING CAME TOO SOON, and Paul found himself somewhat comforted by his ordinary routines. In his own taproom, it wasn't easy to succumb to how terrifying a near-drowning had felt. The memory of ropes at his wrists was harder to shed, but it was because his sleeves brought the association to mind. He'd compromised by rolling them up to his forearms.

What he hadn't told Alastair was, although he hadn't seen any faces, he felt rough hands forcing him into the water and heard two indistinct voices. It had been similar to hearing a conversation through a dense wall, no details, just impressions. One voice shared Alastair's accent, or one similar to it, while the other sounded, funnily enough, a little closer to himself. He would never think Alastair was involved with a decision to kill him, and on the night of Sykes' death, he'd commented he wasn't an indiscriminate killer.

It did not fit with Alastair's innate sweetness, anyway, no matter how he made himself appear to the outside observer. But given the far more distinct vision of flour-dusted men speaking with Edinburgh's tones, Paul had drawn the uncomfortable conclusion that Alastair was the connecting factor between these visions and himself.

It didn't distress him in the sense that he wished to break ties.

But it redoubled his desire to learn more about what Alastair's life had been like before he'd settled in Cromer. Prior to these premonitions, Paul had simply worried his circumstances here were too boring for someone like Alastair, who gave off an air of adventure and spontaneity. Now, he knew Alastair wasn't bored of him or indeed of anything in their days together.

Yet he had more queries than he'd ever possessed before. Considering how Alastair had crashed into his life without any warning at all, that was saying something. Paul didn't think his head had just been turned by a pretty, older man who looked like he could cheerfully bend him in two. He'd been aware of certain things, like Alastair having a criminal past. But if he had wanted to burgle Paul's public house, or somehow hurt him, he could have done so at any point since last September.

He could have done any number of awful things since last autumn.

Paul trusted him, loved him, despite any exasperation. That love came most naturally when they were both exhausted after a long day, when Alastair's voice was soft, deep as strong-brewed coffee, and Paul, who was so tired as to be nearly silent, spoke primarily to say he loved him. Those moments felt more crucial than ever right now. Paul feared that without them, things would fall apart.

"The barriers between things are flimsy this time of year," Benson said, as Paul poured him a liberal measure of gin. The time of day mattered little to Benson when it came to consuming alcohol, even if it did matter to licensing laws.

As it had been prompted by nothing and they'd been in companionable silence until Benson spoke, Paul raised his eyebrows and said, "What's that got to do with the price of fish?"

"Nothing." Most of the gin disappeared in one practiced gulp. "Maybe everything."

"What *things* do you mean?"

"Pardon?"

As ever, Paul didn't know if Benson feigned being scattered, or if he truly was incapable of linear thoughts and subsequent conversation. Patiently, he said, "If *barriers* are flimsy at present, what are the barriers, and what are the things?"

"Haven't you ever heard somebody remark upon the veil between worlds?"

Paul shook his head. No one in his family was able to do what he did, and he'd had no mentors or teachers. He supposed such people existed, but he'd never found one. It had never mattered much to him. He relied more on instinct and his own experience, and didn't think he'd benefit much from instruction or someone telling him he approached things the wrong way. Benson came closest to a preternatural mentor or a teacher, but he was a friend, albeit a strange one. He only talked about it more than others. Unless Paul asked for advice, it didn't seem like it would be supplied as such.

"Not precisely."

"Well, this part of the year," said Benson, "it's more permeable."

At that, Paul knew what Benson meant. His parents had relayed a bevy of regional ghost stories throughout the year, and Halloween wasn't any eerier than any other day in Norfolk, it seemed. "For spirits."

Not that it mattered; Paul couldn't sense the dead. His ability didn't lend itself to them. While Benson had remarked once while drunk that magic, from necromancy to seeing the future to being able to generate fire in one's hands, probably all originated from the same place, he didn't know—nobody knew—if that was true. At the time, since Paul had been extinguishing the edge of a decorative pillow Maeve had set on fire simply by pinching it between her thumb and pointer finger, he hadn't been listening with any attentiveness as Benson mused.

The pillow was only singed, and only in that corner, but Maeve was profoundly embarrassed. Not for the first time, he wanted to ask if she drank so frequently to cope with such a talent, or if it came out more when she'd been drinking. She'd started to come to The Queen Anne just after his mother died, but she was now a regular customer. He did like her, too. It seemed she had no family, or at least no family nearby. She was in her twenties and unmarried, so he secretly felt obligated to be hospitable. He hadn't the heart to make her feel worse than she already appeared to.

Still, after the singed pillow, he did suggest she sit on a stool or refrain from touching anything that could quickly go up in flames.

"For them, yes, but for us as well," Benson said. Paul was about to ask after the us, but Benson continued quickly. "Those of us who see and talk to them."

Paul was about to remind Benson he wasn't a necromancer; he wasn't even sure if he was a witch, though if one felt all preternatural power came from one source, then he was. Before he could, Benson went on to say, "Those of us who see the future."

"Shouldn't have ever told you," Paul said. Still, he smiled.

"Had any strong ones, of late?"

Trying to tell if Benson knew already, or if he was only very good at feeling magical tides, so to speak, Paul narrowed his eyes. "If I have, what do you think you'd..." The front door creaked slightly. Used to it, Paul assumed it was Molly, or another of the maids, or possibly one of the three customers who'd paid for a few days' lodging. They were all naturalists who knew each other, and were apparently keen on the seaside. If not any of them, either of The Queen Anne's more long-term lodgers came and went as they pleased.

"What the *fuck?*"

Benson lazily tilted his head in the direction of the question that cut across Paul's thoughts, and Paul quieted. For his part, he had to stifle a laugh.

It *was* Molly. He was well used to Alastair's penchant for expletives, but he had never heard her say something so coarse. Expecting nothing more than perhaps a strange spider or some such thing to have pushed her to it, he waited for her hurried footsteps to come into the taproom. He was usually startled by spiders, and they could elicit a similar response from him. Particularly if they appeared out of seemingly nowhere.

"I am sorry, Mr. Apollyon," she said, as she entered.

"It's all right." He waited for her to elaborate. They'd all learned Molly was too shy to be pushed into talking. While she caught her breath, he noted her cheeks were paler than usual.

"Was someone shouting?" Alastair came from the corridor in a silent rush that was impressive for a man with his build; he'd been in the cellar taking some inventory of the stock.

Still rather amused by Molly's outburst, Paul watched as her usual nerves around Alastair warred with whatever had just happened to make her say *fuck* aloud. He couldn't blame her for going speechless when Alastair was in a room, and had wondered several times if it was due more to attraction than actual fear. He would never ask, of course.

"Me," she said, after she cleared her throat. "I shouted."

Kindly, Alastair asked her, "Why? You look unharmed. Unsettled, but unharmed."

Benson remained quiet, for which Paul was thankful. Poor Molly might run from the taproom if Alastair and

Benson, each so unconventional and intense in his own manner, were both talking to her.

"I am, sir," she said, pushing aside a bit of deep brown hair that escaped its pins. "Unharmed, I mean to say. Unsettled... well, that's a way to put it."

Unruffled, Alastair replied, "What's happened, then? And I'm not 'sir.' Just... Mr. Gow, if you must." Amused when Alastair seemed to struggle with accepting that form of address, too, Paul hid a smile when he added, "I'd prefer Alastair, but I know that's not the done thing."

"Oh, sir—Mr. Gow," Molly said. "I wouldn't."

"No, I know," said Alastair. "If it helps..." he glanced briefly at Paul. "I just work here, too."

To that, even shy Molly dimpled, almost smirked, slightly. Benson, meanwhile, snorted. She was seventeen, if Paul recalled correctly, and not ignorant of what went on around her. "I know you work, sir, but I don't know about the *just.*" She might have been startled by her own boldness, because then she went rather pink in contrast to how pale she'd been upon coming in.

"Yes, well," Alastair said, not without a certain twinkle in his eyes, "if we could leave that to the side... what happened?"

Irresistibly, Paul recalled the conversation he'd seen between the younger and older men. In this moment, seeing how Alastair dealt with somebody in clear distress, Paul couldn't think he would be a *bad* father. The notion saddened him, and not because there was anything wrong with Alastair being a father. Men like them just didn't find themselves in the situation of fatherhood through simple routes. Alastair must have been lonely.

As he watched Alastair watch Molly with kind concern,

Paul wanted to ask why he'd never seen fit to share this part of himself. Instead of giving into the urge, he said to Molly, "Take your time."

She switched her large, dark eyes to him, and his words seemed to do the trick to get her to say what was wrong. "Begging your pardon, because this will sound strange." She drew a long breath before saying, "But somebody's gone and put a dead bird on the door. I was going to polish the handle, and there it was."

5

———

In fact, it was not just any bird. It was a modestly sized crow. Alastair frowned at it, hooking his thumbs into both his pockets for a moment. Instinctively, he kept himself between the crow and Paul, though Paul was still trying to examine the sorry thing more closely under the morning's cloud-covered light. Covertly, Alastair tried to take stock of their surroundings without his notice, trying to use his peripheral vision without moving his head.

He wanted to make certain they weren't watched, but was enough of a pragmatist to know he couldn't promise they remained unobserved. Particularly by any unsavory parties whose work it was to escape notice. Though, by that same token, he would bet on any seaside grandmother having more acumen than hired hands did. Maybe they only had to worry about the eyes of elderly neighbors, but his gut told him to be careful.

They'd left Molly inside with Benson, who was being reasonably normal and had offered to make her a cup of tea.

What the tea would have in it, nobody could guarantee, but the offer was kind enough.

Paul's breath was on the back of his neck, warm and familiar. "Well, I'll echo Molly. What the fuck?" Alastair barely heard him. Paul spoke normally, quietly compared to most people, yet in a perfectly usual manner for himself.

But his mind was elsewhere, split between Benson's mention of the Adairs—their money—and events of over ten years ago. He had worked hard to move past them. To have this converge in Cromer, when he'd believed it to be behind him, was troublesome. He took a halting breath. "I'll take care of it."

"What do you mean? It's clearly dead."

"I'll toss it in the sea. It's still early. Nobody has to notice this."

As though there wasn't a dead crow nailed to his public house's door and it was only a notice or advertisement, Paul said, almost coolly, "What does it mean?" As Alastair just sighed, he said, "To you."

First, Alastair tried disavowal. "Nothing." Though it might send an intelligible message to him, he wished to decode it and answer without involving Paul. Explaining would involve him, for he wouldn't be content to be idle, and he might send Alastair away.

"My father had some rows with locals now and again. Mother wasn't everyone's cup of tea." Paul scoffed. "The Mills don't care for us Apollyons... my grandfather knew more about that old grudge than anyone, but I never asked him why."

Wordlessly, resigned, Alastair turned to him, his beautiful man who could cut through layers of evasiveness like a knife sliced through a soft millefeuille. "Point being?" He shouldn't have assumed Paul would let it go. But it agitated him. He'd prefer Paul just said what he meant. Normally, he did. The rather stubborn words and, for him, the verbosity, were new.

"Nobody has *ever* stuck a deceased bird to the door. We haven't even received nasty letters or notes. And we've had a few rumors—someone said my mother was a witch, once. They just picked the wrong Apollyon."

"Let me take care of it," Alastair muttered. He meant dispose of the bird. "And then—"

Paul didn't let him finish. "Then what?"

"I'll come back inside, and we can—"

"I won't let you seduce your way out of talking," said Paul, with a voice that didn't carry. Though there was the faintest smile on his face, his eyes were serious. The hazel caught what diffuse light there was, and it might've driven a more artistic man to poetry.

Alastair suspected there were only a handful of times more he could sidestep telling the truth. His control was eroding. But apparently, so were the stable, safe circumstances he'd been cultivating since last September. "What a shame. It would be fun."

You're not meant for this kind of life, said a tempting thought. He'd had it before. While it had been correct about his marriage and his attempt to be an ordinary man with a wife and child, he didn't want it to be right about the life he now had.

"I don't think I have much to do with this poor thing being here," said Paul. Discreetly, as though the touch meant nothing and was one that could occur between friends, he put his hand on Alastair's upper arm, resting it on his shirtsleeve.

Alastair had been so startled by Molly's shout that he'd come up from the cellar without his jumper and hat. He imagined, if anyone *was* observing him, he looked quite the eccentric sight, dressed just in an old blackish-gray shirt with chipped buttons, and faded black twill trousers that had fared slightly better than the shirt. His hair was only partially bundled back.

At least you're not barefoot. Some of the fishermen and sailors might know what the pig and the rooster tattooed on the top of either foot meant, but nobody else would. "Does it frighten you?" He endeavored to ignore the choking sensation that crept up his throat.

"No." Paul lightly squeezed his arm.

Alastair glanced at the crow again. He said, "Perhaps it should."

"Go ahead and throw it into the water," said Paul, "as you're rather good at that kind of disposal." He did smile, then, making reference to Sykes' knife being disposed in the same way. Alastair snorted. On balance, it wasn't so long ago that he was running about, trying to lose Muriel's drunken father, who'd mistakenly assumed Alastair had compromised Muriel's honor. Little did Sykes know, a woman called Abigail had already done it. All Alastair had done was carry their letters.

He loved love, he liked Muriel, and he hadn't liked Sykes. The only reason he'd even been involved with the bastard was business. Their transactions weren't immense, just having to do with certain liquors being exchanged without any duty or official records. The days of grandiose highwaymen and pirates were well behind them, though Paul sometimes teased that Alastair looked like one. "I just like to throw things."

With a nod, Paul murmured, coming closer to his ear, "When you're done with that, you can come back and tell me what you're trying so diligently not to tell me."

Alastair shivered. Paul might not want to be seduced in lieu of being told the truth. But he'd gladly let Paul seduce *him* if it meant he could disregard old problems coming back to the fore. "After I've washed my hands."

"Of course," said Paul, backing away lest they attract attention for being so close.

Luckily, there'd been no passersby as they stood and contemplated the crow. Alastair assumed he'd just leap in front of the door and take it off, hiding it behind his back, if anyone needed to enter via this primary entrance for customers.

But one never knew who could be peering out their windows. He thought again of Cromer grannies. It was fine for The Queen Anne's landlord to have a reputation for favoring men, even for him to keep a lover. But it was quite another matter for him to kiss that lover outside a private room. For one thing, Paul was very well regarded among the elderly set, grannies and granddads alike, and they would fret he'd come to harm.

Breathing on his neck often resulted in kissing at some point. He sighed and said, "Go on, angel." Paul had brought a rough sack out with him, thinking as always with some pragmatism. He wordlessly held it out just under the crow, leaving Alastair between himself and the door. "Thank you."

Careful not to jostle it too much out of respect for a creature that had just been alive, Alastair worked the cheap twine that was wrapped around its neck to fix it to the handle. He didn't like the cool feathers under his fingertips. Then he loosened the nail pinning one of its wings.

With a sad, soft thump, the crow fell into the sack and Alastair dropped the twine after it. He was forming an idea of who'd left the gift, his conjecture strengthened by Benson's message. Even Paul's vision of drowning might be an added reason to think along the lines he was, although he did not want to follow that through to any possible future conclusions.

In truth, if what he was starting to suspect had any merit, the sender wasn't the most frightful person and that was a small blessing.

Lucas was just one of the surliest people, and as a boy of eleven, he'd been taken in by a man known only as Old Ross who boasted he was from a long line of brutes. He was by trade a butcher, and gloried in such delights as stringing crows to his enemies' doors or smearing their thresholds with mysterious, mulish red substances most resembling congealed blood. It was suspected his shop was a front for something else, though nobody could prove any theories, and Lucas never breathed a word about it even after he'd grown up and been on his own.

Since Old Ross was a bit of a radge, no one pressed Lucas much about what living with him had been like. Lucas had, however, possessed a slight penchant for doing one of the same things as his former guardian. There'd been several times when he'd left a corvid by way of voicing his displeasure or to intimidate, although he did not seem to favor the practice past his youth. Nobody of their circle condoned it, and so he'd given it up.

As these thoughts flitted through his mind, Alastair only felt most viscerally that he had crossed Lucas, perhaps with the mistaken belief this wouldn't matter for long, if at all. It hadn't been intentional or malicious. Whether Lucas might know more than he'd said about the empty room in the Adair house had always been a lingering question, one to which he had no definitive answer, merely suspicions.

Frowning, he lingered near Paul and the door. It seemed too convenient that someone else would take up such a macabre habit near enough for Alastair to take notice. On the other hand, he might be ascribing another person's ghoulish behavior to Lucas. Norfolk was, as many of its inhabitants liked to tease, considered weird. Though, he could not say it was a grisly place, particularly not when he had witnessed a bevy of dreadful things elsewhere. Perhaps everywhere was or could be, for the likes of him.

Paul said, and Alastair did not know how long he had been standing motionless, restless in his own mind, "You should go. I want to know about whatever you are thinking behind that scowl. But it would be ideal to make everything look as normal as possible before people really start milling about."

"No, you're right." With a parting warm glance, he turned to go in the direction of the promenade, and made sure to carry his bizarre cargo like it was nothing at all. It didn't weigh much, and he was confident he could finish his errand without arousing any suspicion. Tradesmen, fishermen, and the like were up, but he doubted he'd see anybody on their leisure.

When his boots met the beach, he reflected upon how correct Paul often turned out to be. It was still alien to allow for vulnerability, for someone else to be right, even if he suspected it might serve him well.

"I ALMOST EXPECTED you to bolt until bedtime," said Paul, as Alastair came through the empty taproom door about thirty minutes later. He regretted it instantly; Alastair's expression went from hurt to shuttered in a moment. "Sorry," he added, and meant it, though he did still have the sense Alastair was ready to run. He wanted to get to the bottom of the matter at hand, not wound him.

"No, I deserved that." With a fluidity of movement that was still somewhat surprising due to his stature, Alastair crossed the room, came to the bar, and sat atop it. He was always soundless unless he wished to make noise, and he was graceful in a pugilistic way, reminiscent of a spry boxer rather than a dancer. More than once, Paul wanted to ask if Alastair might teach him to fight, but there'd never been a moment for him to bring it up.

Paul wasn't serving anyone, and Benson had drifted to one of the common areas tucked near the stairs to smoke his pipe in peace.

Now he was taking the opportunity, as he often did, to make sure all was in order and the bar itself was clean before afternoon and evening. By then, he'd have no time to do so. The low ceilings would be sheltering a vociferous throng of mostly regular customers, the beams overhead bearing witness to all manner of daily, ongoing conversations over pints and puffing pipes.

"If you were anybody else, I'd never allow that."

"But I'm not anybody else," said Alastair. He winked, and Paul eyed him, trying to ascertain if he was evading again.

Deciding to employ a line of conversation he thought would work because it was about his own mortality, Paul said, "Have you washed?" Alastair might've come from the back, in which case, there was a basin and soap just opposite the kitchen door. "If my life is suddenly under threat, the least you can do is have clean hands in my establishment." He didn't actually believe he was under threat, though the thought of drowning hadn't left him. If, indeed, it ever would.

The words did their trick. "You're not under threat," said Alastair. He scowled as quickly as he'd winked. "If anything, I think I'm supposed to be. And yes, my hands are clean."

"I'm not exactly happy with you being under threat, either. If you are."

"I can handle it."

"So can I."

"I don't want you to."

"Fine, if you don't want to talk about that, we can at least speak about the letters again." Off Alastair's mutinous look, he said, "I'm not trying to nag you, though it may seem otherwise." Paul glanced at the doorway leading to the entry and the little corner with a desk he used to write receipts and handle documents. The Queen Anne had, over the years, settled at charmingly odd angles, so the door was just slightly askew. Much like his thoughts at present.

Out of general caution, he lowered his voice and tried not to plead. "It's been over a year. You know me better than anyone ever has." That feeling of being known brought him serenity, while it seemed to bring Alastair agitation. "But I daresay I know you better than you'd like."

He paused, trying to read the emotions surfacing on Alastair's face. They were more varied than he would have thought. Gone was mutiny, replaced by what Paul could only name as longing. Then love. Then fear. When Alastair did not halt him, he added, "What are you afraid of? It must be something about me."

Alastair eyed his own boots. So Paul said, at a loss, "I can't see things you don't want me to." *Well, that isn't strictly true.* He knew Alastair would not like hearing that he'd seen those flour-dusted men. He shook his head a little. "I can't read your mind. I'd hate being able to. I *can* sort of glean what state you're in, sometimes, but you already know that."

Falling quiet, he let them simply breathe for a few moments. There was no need to belabor the point. They both knew about Paul's sense of certain phantom colors and smells around people. Preternatural signatures, little tells that might indicate if someone was ill, pleased, melancholy, feeling well, in love. It wasn't always there for him.

Thank fuck for that. His life would be a cacophony of sensations otherwise.

Then Alastair said something unexpected, although Paul had not been certain he would say anything. Compared to other times they'd spoken about his personal matters, that he had stayed in the taproom was progress. "I'm afraid of losing you." The soft sentence was almost forced, not in the sense that it was contrived or meant to distract him. It was just strenuously delivered, as though doing so had cost some effort.

"Pardon?" Paul hadn't once thought that he would break ties over their present stalemate of communication. He frowned. He also wouldn't have dreamed Alastair was worried about it, not looking as he did or being as confident as he was.

"If you knew what sort of person I am, you'd tell me to go."

That was absurd to Paul and he almost said as much, but instead he took care not to sound too dismissive. "I know what sort of person you are." He watched Alastair's hands on the bar, flat on either side of his thighs and so oddly still. The fingerless gloves he'd favored when they met were now often abandoned in private. More of his tattoos were exposed. Some were delicate stars and decorative lines, while a peony featured on the back of his left hand, and Paul felt he was a tapestry of moments in ink.

"You don't."

Tentatively, Paul said, "I would if you told me. I'm trusting what I've seen of you."

The sort of man who put himself at risk to help two women run away couldn't be a bad one, for a start. As though agreeing with Paul's words and thought, the inherited canary chittered softly from its nearby perch on a trug basket near the hearth. He'd let it out, as always, when he first rose that morning. It was an accord they had reached with the bird. Freedom upon waking.

"I love that," said Alastair. He might as well have been saying, *I love you.* He had said so, numerous times. Paul found it a little funny that he could so easily say something that most men regarded as difficult, even when their affections' recipients were more acceptable.

Moistening his lips with the tip of his tongue before he spoke, Paul made another decision concerning strategic conversation. He would talk about the young man called James and see what happened. "The vision I had when I was awake. When you came upon me."

Fidgeting a little, Alastair said, "Yes?"

"I wanted to tell you what it was about, but the second one sort of took precedence."

Something about Paul's face must have tugged at Alastair's instincts, for his eyes narrowed as though he tried to see under a bright sky. "Understandable. That second one was absolutely grim. I'm still worried it'll happen."

"Just don't let me near large bodies of water."

"We do live by the sea. Won't take my eyes from you for the rest of my life, if that's what it takes."

"I don't doubt it. But the first one..."

"I'm hoping it was dull."

"Keep hoping," said Paul. He reached for Alastair's left hand and covered the peony with his palm. He felt there was a slim chance Alastair would go mute and run in response to what he said next.

"Paul?" Alastair's gaze went to their hands, and his tone wasn't relaxed by any means. Still, he didn't move his hand away. It didn't so much as twitch.

As gently as he could, for he took no true pleasure in asking it, he said, "Who is James?"

If nothing else, Alastair was incredibly stalwart under pressure. Paul already knew, but his reaction to this question reconfirmed it. His eyes didn't even waver when he asked, "Have you spoken with Benson?"

"No." Part of him was relieved. This wasn't denial or dismissal. "Not at all."

"Of course you haven't," said Alastair. He was, if Paul heard him correctly, rueful. "My seer wouldn't need to do that."

"Yes, yours," said Paul. "There's almost nothing you could do to dissuade me from *being* yours." Short of cruelty and matters of abuse, Paul knew he was lost. He'd been lost from the start, the very moment when Alastair appeared in a huff.

He was unprepared for what happened next. Alastair turned his own hand over and entwined their fingers. With the same gesture and a look of hunger, he pulled Paul as close as he could stand against the back of the bar. Alastair's long legs were still over the opposite side, the side that faced customers, so their bodies were almost positioned like they might be on a tête-à-tête.

Except, instead of both of them being seated, Paul stood facing Alastair's slightly twisted torso. Their lower halves were still separated by the bar, and Paul found himself disappointed. He tried to be grateful. He didn't think even The Queen Anne in all its eccentricity could survive rumors of its landlord being ravished on his own bar. *He* might not even survive rumors of that kind if someone malicious said something incriminating to interested authorities.

But he wouldn't have minded, if that was what Alastair wanted to do. At least, he wouldn't have minded at this exact moment.

"Perhaps that loyalty should cause you more concern, angel."

"It causes *you* too much," Paul retorted, his chin tilted so he could better study Alastair's face. From so close together, and with Alastair seated as he was on the bar top, he saw every new bit of gray and silver in his dark hair, and the unshaven stubble on his chin. He studied the encroaching lines on his mouth and forehead. "You have me, so act accordingly. I'm your equal, aren't I?"

Full moments passed, charged ones that had Paul aching for a kiss. "Fuck," Alastair said at last. "Of course you are. I should think you're better than I'll ever be."

"You're always my equal," Alastair continued. "If not... more. Better."

"Might have fooled me."

Looking into his eyes, Alastair sighed and looked away. He *was* expertly evasive when it came to his private thoughts. Even now, he had been expecting more talk of the crow and of men sending alarming messages through a sad, dead creature. It had first come from a story, or stories, he was sure, the use of a bird's corpse to do such a thing. He'd heard of bad witches doing something similar with papers strewn in trees by kirkyards. They'd write curses on the papers, supposedly, and then some devout Christian would touch it or read it and carry the malice through the contact.

The crows were similar to the curses. They said, *I'm watching you and I found you* or *I'm coming for you and I'll make you hurt.*

Instead of talking about this, he was asked to talk about the thing that confused and dismayed him more than such threats. He could defend himself against external hazards, yet he had to stand behind his choices. That, he had more trouble with.

But it still felt interconnected, for without the Adairs and their money, he'd have had little to send to James. He had done rather well with it over the years, investing and saving. So he was perhaps not wealthy by the wealthy's standards, but he was financially stable, which was far more than his ancestors could say. He tried to answer Paul's initial question, but had to focus on dust motes drifting in the taproom's haphazard light in order to begin.

"James is…"

"Your stepson," said Paul, quietly, when the sentence lingered unfinished for a little too long.

Instead of being irked that he'd said the words, Alastair was glad. He felt helped, as though part of the burden of revelation had been carried for him. He was also wrestling with the elements of preternatural things within all of this, Benson's words and Paul's visions. He couldn't quiet the instinct that something important had arrived. "Yes."

Paul stroked the inside of his palm with his thumb, their hands still entwined. "You were married, or are." It was hard to tell how he actually felt about it, but he sounded rather small. "Which I suppose is all right. It's not as though we could ever marry."

For all he kept from Paul, he still felt as though Paul could see everything about him, and would make connections others couldn't about who he was. This intuitive quality allured him as much as it unnerved him. He did worry that Paul would still choose to go on without him.

Yet he had said he wouldn't. That granted Alastair courage. He forced himself to swallow, and met Paul's eyes.

Briefly, he shook his head. "I'm a widower. I *was* married." He knew, they both would know, that anybody could live bigamously, obscuring or neglecting one union to in effect have another. Divorce was costly and often complicated where it was even possible, not at all a promised option. Alastair possessed no particular view on anybody deciding to live such a double life. Some saw it as scandalous. He saw it as an action, one of many somebody could take.

Nonetheless, he needed Paul to know he wasn't secondary.

"Oh." Paul released a breath. His jaw relaxed minutely.

An ache rose in Alastair's chest; he knew he'd hurt Paul with this and there was no way to deny it. "I..." he didn't know where to start, or rather, how to proceed. Now that the topic had been opened, he couldn't decide what to do or how to elaborate. His hand was trembling, and Paul could surely feel it, holding hands as they were. *All* of him was trembling with nerves. Perhaps he should run about outside for a few minutes and return with more composure.

"I did think you'd had a more complicated life than me," said Paul, with a weak chuckle.

"Well, I'm not a seer," he offered. It was one complication he didn't have.

"It's not all it's said to be." With kind directness, Paul took him back to the matter at hand. "Right, so, you *were* married."

Alastair nodded. "I knew I liked men. But my mother wanted to see me married, and my wife, or fiancée, and I were friends. We thought to help each other."

It felt like an entirely different lifetime. He suspected his mother had never admitted where his true affections were. Father made remarks to her about it, but that was different from it being acknowledged. While she was clever with story-telling and keeping a family going on almost nothing, she wasn't terribly good at standing up for herself.

She barely managed to with Father, who never struck her too terribly in front of Alastair. He'd heard worse than he'd seen. She had wanted Alastair married to get him away. Father respected marriage beyond having a trade or an education; when young Alastair mentioned leaving home for work, it was always dismissed as fanciful.

Leaving was situated within the idea of being married, of being a man and having a family to provide for. It was that, or go join the pansies in a monastery, his father had said, amidst big guffaws. He could recognize the derision for what it was now, though he had not as a boy.

He wanted to see me married off because he liked the thought of me being so miserable.

If nothing else, marrying Evie had been worth it because he then lived with a friend instead of a browbeaten mother and an odious father. Money had not been a problem for them; he'd still been situated in petty criminal circles, then events with the Adairs let him ease back from that life.

"You must have been quite young when you wed." Paul's voice held sympathy and drew him back to the present. "Molly's age, or younger."

"We were." *I was barely older than James is, now.* It wasn't so out of the ordinary and he didn't feel sorry for himself due to his youth. But he could admit he had much more knowledge of life now than he'd had then.

Paul tilted his head, and Alastair could tell he was going to ask what would be considered an impertinent question in polite company. He welcomed it. "Did she have her son, already?"

He couldn't help his smile. "No, although I would have married her. She fell pregnant after we married. Not by me, obviously."

Alastair wanted to add he'd done little with any women past kissing them. But it didn't fit the tenor of their conversation. Besides, he had always felt the need to hide that fact with ribald talk. He never said anything derogatory about women, but with some bravado, he had let others think he'd been with quite a few. Anybody who didn't know him well usually believed that he preferred them.

It made things easier, and he'd flirted his way out of a few tight spots. He'd even tried to maintain the lies with his father, though he had not been successful. The older he became, the less he clung to the pretense, and Evie, having Arthur, gave her blessing to Alastair keeping lovers. She hadn't seen anything wrong with what he was.

Appearing to think about something, his expression going a little inward, Paul nodded. Then, he murmured, "That does make sense. I saw two men in my vision."

"Did the younger one have greenish eyes?"

Nodding again, Paul said, "Yes. They were talking amongst themselves, and they both wore aprons. Sort of covered in flour."

In spite of his nerves and the seriousness of the discussion, Alastair felt his smile slip into more of a grin. He was still shaken by trying to navigate this very new openness. But it wasn't easy to be cross with Arthur, or with the way James took so much after Evie.

"Arthur is James' father. He's a baker. Evie—she was my

wife—she met Arthur not three months into us being married. She says to me, a while after they had been carrying on, 'I think I might love him, Aly.' I could see it." He smiled, recalling the wonder that had been in her expression. "I said, 'Christ, don't let me stop you, then.' She didn't."

When Paul laughed, Alastair felt rather more at ease. He added, "Which was very clever of her, because he's a better man than me."

"I don't know about that."

Alastair murmured, leaving that aside for the moment, "My own family was poor. But I had income from..." Paul's eyes widened just a little, perhaps out of eagerness over receiving more personal information from him. He wasn't ready to give it. "Various ventures. Marriage granted Evie more freedom."

Paul squeezed his hand with a pleasant amount of pleasure, and leaned across the top of the bar, closer to him. "Clearly you didn't begrudge her."

"No. We decided it wouldn't be best for us to part. It would've given her a certain reputation, among other things. Besides, as I said, we were friends. An affair with a man she loved was the better option."

"He accepted the situation?"

"Yes," said Alastair, "he's a rare sort of man, I think."

"I'm glad. I see from your face that she was happy."

Though he'd loved stories of romance since boyhood, Evie and Arthur exemplified it. Love had made her incandescent, and Arthur wasn't frightened of her unorthodox situation. While many might dismiss such a notion, Alastair believed Arthur loved Evie enough to accept it. Trying to force her to take measures she didn't wish to, like running away, wasn't part of his love.

It shouldn't have been, especially when Alastair posed him no threat in that regard. There had been many a night when Alastair went to a public house or took a very long walk to give them privacy, and many a night when Evie didn't come back until morning because she'd been in Arthur's flat over his bakery. When James came along, they did try to behave more decorously. He glanced at Paul. The new silence that spread between the two of them wasn't tense, to his relief. It didn't come naturally to him not to interject or make a quip, but he refrained.

At length, when Paul's thumb had stopped stroking his palm, he asked, "When you saw Arthur and James, what were they doing?"

"Only talking. The younger one, James, he did seem bitter." Paul regarded him. "He's certainly taking your money."

"Oh, I know," said Alastair, past feeling any measure of surprise that Paul had been able to conclude whom his letters were going to, "it leaves my accounts, so it's going somewhere." Setting up bank accounts had been a fascinating experience. He'd had fewer tattoos then, which made it easier to appear respectable, and he simply forged the requisite documents and references.

But these visions would never cease to be a marvel to him, despite growing up with a mother who filled him with all sorts of fantastical tales. He couldn't even be angry that something Paul saw had exposed him. In truth, he should have expected it was a possibility and divulged more before he became too scared to bare himself.

Now, knowing that Paul had seen nothing but an incredibly real scenario, he was even more worried about the one in which Paul had drowned.

"Why are you sending it to him? He seems to have work. And he said something about a house." Paul didn't seem to mean it in a scathing way. He merely sounded curious. "And you're still perched on the bar. Can we sit? My feet hurt. Not used to standing so still for this long."

"Oh." Releasing his hand with some reluctance, Alastair hopped back to the floor. "Of course we can."

When Paul came around, Alastair didn't dare kiss him and interrupt the moment, though he wanted to. Instead, he preceded Paul to a bench-like thing that might have started its life as a pew. He hadn't asked and he hadn't been inside enough churches to say. Positioned near the unlit fire and strewn with jewel-toned cushions, it was much more comfortable than it looked.

Face upturned to watch Paul's approach; he paused before saying why he sent money to James. Some of it was guilt, but he wasn't ashamed of feeling guilty. He was just caught by the beauty of the man coming to sit with him, as he had been numerous times. Slight, graceful, and generally neater than most people even if he didn't care enough about fashion to do the done things. But Paul had a presence beyond any of that; it always called to him.

Paul sat down soundlessly, settling close. He'd bought a new jasmine soap recently; it suited him, wafting discreetly wherever he went and leaving a particularly carnal impression upon Alastair whenever he was nearby.

Barely distracted by the front door opening and closing, followed by light footsteps in the foyer, Alastair said, "I'm sending it because it's the least I can do for shattering his life. I knew what I was doing when I left; I didn't think it would be easy on him." This was the thorniest thing to talk about; it required admission of his own culpability. But it was interrupted before he could really begin.

"Paul?" It was Miss Garland, a kindred spirit in many ways. She dispensed with any use of Mr. Apollyon if The Queen Anne wasn't busy, but she wasn't exactly the most proper of women to begin with.

Alastair smiled at him. "Don't think I'm happy to halt the conversation." He was rather shocked to discover that he wasn't, as though once he had started, he needed to release everything he was thinking.

Paul said, "Don't think you can forever." He didn't rise from the pew, and looked at Miss Garland, who drifted into the taproom with the grace of someone crossing a grand ballroom. "As long as you haven't come bearing a dead bird, I am glad to see you."

6

____

She gazed at him as though he'd spoken in tongues. "A dead bird?"

He beamed at her. "Never mind. We've had something of a strange morning."

Miss Garland's eyes went from him, to Alastair, then to him again. "Are you engaged?"

"Not in the way church or law would recognize, no," said Paul, offering a quip. "How can I help? You are rarely by so early in the morning." It wasn't early for him, but it was for her. Anything before noon was considered early within her social calendar, though she said she enjoyed mornings when she could be awake for them.

"Oh," she said dismissively, pulling up a wooden chair near the old pew he and Alastair presently sat upon, "I've just finished with my appointment over at Red Lion. He fell back asleep after he paid, and I left because I heard some gossip last night that may pertain to you."

The Red Lion was larger than The Queen Anne. His parents had always referenced it, as had Grandfather. He thought the relationship between the two establishments was friendly, but it had been an age since he'd been inside himself. "From your appointment?"

"Goodness, no, he was so dull."

Alastair chuckled and Paul smirked over at him. No doubt, she had a bevy of dull clients. He had little experience with people who were comfortable enough to afford the best of everything, but he had a bit, and Miss Garland's clientele always tended to be on the richer side of life. They were always less observant than Paul expected, though he tried not to comment much on their actual intelligence. Miss Garland would know better than him, and she was always entertaining when she did comment.

With the exception of Benson, she didn't bother with anybody who couldn't pay handsomely. He and Alastair were still trying to grasp what Miss Garland and Benson actually had, whether it was friendly or romantic or just business. And Benson was, so far as these things went with older men, good looking in Paul's opinion. Or he would be if he bothered.

Miss Garland straightened her puce skirts. "Two Scottish gentlemen at the bar last night were talking about The Queen Anne."

"Not strange to come down from Scotland," said Paul.

"No," she said, "but these two were so loud. I was intrigued, you see, if only because I'm nosy. So I came a little closer, and one of them, a lithe man with reddish hair, he took to me right then."

It was easy for Paul to imagine. She was beautiful, with gray eyes and glossy dark hair. He knew many men were immediately attracted to her, and watching it happen a few times in the taproom had been diverting enough. "Can't say that's surprising."

"Thank you," she said primly, "but since I was there for someone else, I had to respectfully decline. I may go back tonight; they said they had business to attend to and they might be here for some time." She regarded Paul and Alastair for a moment, seeming to collect her thoughts.

She didn't appear agitated, merely rather perplexed. "But what was strange was, the one who spoke most to me, a Mr. Lucas... he didn't seem as keen on asking questions about me or appointments. They almost always go right into that, and he didn't at all." Then she sat back in her chair, apparently still puzzling it over.

From Paul's left, Alastair stiffened. It couldn't have been because of the talk of Miss Garland's profession. Anyway, Paul could guess that Alastair had heard far more explicit things than Miss Garland ever said. He had certainly heard more explicit things from Paul's own lips, and they'd generally come by way of Miss Garland's naughty books before being bolstered with Paul's love for him.

"What did he ask about, then?" Paul said.

"You."

"Me?" The only Scottish person he knew was currently seated next to him and seemed as taut as a pulled bowstring.

"Well, not you precisely," she said, shaking her head and frowning, "but as I said, they'd been mentioning here. When I said the landlord was my friend, Mr. Lucas showed even more charm. Said they'd tried to stay here but couldn't, which I knew wasn't the case. You have rooms available, so why would you turn them away?"

Confused, Paul said, "They never came here."

"That's the thing," said Miss Garland, "they were lying and not making much sense about it. I don't mean to say they were so drunk they couldn't make *any* sense. So I merely sat there and let them talk. I was early for my appointment, after all, and if I could schedule another one with that Mr. Lucas while he was here, why not? He does seem a little beneath my usual clientele, but not without *any* money."

There it was again: Alastair did flinch, just a hair, whenever she said Mr. Lucas.

Looking at him sidelong, Paul tried to judge his expression. It wasn't especially troubled, but his jaw was indeed clenched.

More secrets, then? He added this Mr. Lucas to his mental list of topics to dredge up.

"The odd thing is, they were less interested in you the more they spoke to me." She inclined her head toward Alastair. "But they knew all about him." Her eyes met Alastair's. "They knew you were here."

"They knew we're..." Paul swallowed. "They knew we're together?"

It felt worse to have strangers knowing his personal business than it did anyone local on the high street, or Maeve as she set fire to something, or Benson, who would always be an outsider anyway. A good subset of Cromer's residents seemed to know, but he understood that group and took care not to let the knowledge go much further. He was prosaic and thought many folk didn't much care, yet he was not optimistic enough to assume it could never pose an issue.

Miss Garland hastened to reassure him. "I don't think so, no. If they do, they didn't remark upon it." Paul wasn't reassured by much. But she looked again at Alastair. "They asked if I knew a Mr. Gow, and I said I did, mostly to see if they would tell me why they asked."

"You could have lied," said Alastair.

A little cowed, Miss Garland said, "They didn't seem dangerous."

Because he had sounded so dry, almost angry, Paul did turn his head to see him properly then. If anyone knew dangerous, it was Miss Garland, whose safety depended greatly on her sense of a man. She was not working the streets as such, and her world was far removed from the rookeries of London, but she still needed to maintain her wits.

Alastair looked serious as the grave. Placing a hand on his upper thigh, knowing present company wouldn't be scandalized in the slightest, he said, "Alastair?"

Rather than calm him, it produced the opposite effect. Under his hand, Alastair's muscle went tight. His face was relatively serene, and his body was positioned in a normal, conversational way, but under all of that, he seemed quite ready to bolt. Paul knew Miss Garland was an excellent hand at reading anyone, and this moment proved no different.

She said, with some apology in her tone, "Neither said. They just exchanged a bit of a look. Mr. Lucas chuckled in a satisfied sort of way."

It wasn't two more seconds beyond her words before Alastair rose to his feet, and let Paul's hand fall to the nearest pillow on the pew, one the color of a ripe orange. Paul squeezed the pillow as he looked up, not fearful of what Alastair was going to do, but feeling somewhat heartsick at this moment. It was bigger than both of them, larger than a dead wife and stepson left behind. Those things were on the edges, yet he sensed more was to come.

"If you'll both excuse me," was all Alastair said. It was said politely, quietly. But Paul knew under the facade, there was a hum of fear. He went to the door leading to the entryway, his expression composed enough. Yet when Paul focused on the otherworldly currents around him, the unreal green hovering at their edges was laced with black.

That blackness, paired with the forced look of serenity on his face, made Paul venture a small, "Wait."

Alastair said softly, over his shoulder, "I'll be back. Don't worry." Then he was gone. The front door closed firmly, and Paul looked rather helplessly at Miss Garland.

She looked back at him, mystified. "I didn't mean to..."

Rising carefully, for his body had gone tense, Paul halted her words. "You didn't do anything. I appreciate you coming to say something." His head felt too small. For the first time since he was very young, he wished he couldn't see anything extraordinary. Perhaps all of this, such as it was, would have been easier if he knew as little as possible about it.

But he already knew as little as Alastair wished him to. Resigned, he tried to tell himself that was acceptable, and maybe it was the price of love.

THOUGH HIS FIRST thought was to go directly to The Red Lion, Alastair realized it was still before noon—the morning felt like it'd dragged for months—and he didn't actually want to put himself in Lucas' path so quickly. Some time had passed since they'd seen each other, and he doubted he was the same person Lucas had known. He might come off as no threat at all, these days, but what he wished to do was pummel the man into the nearest tabletop, and that wasn't advisable.

For all he believed Lucas wouldn't bother to do much, clearly he had done enough to find him and come here. He knew Adair had rerouted family heirlooms, artifacts, treasure, to Alastair in the form of money. More money than he'd known what to do with, but it was certainly enough to keep him solvent and still send some off to James.

"Fuck," he mumbled.

He wanted to shout it, but didn't dare in the middle of the street. Taking several deep breaths, he attempted to quiet his thoughts. He hadn't meant to double-cross anyone. Far from it. In fact, he hadn't meant to be rewarded at all, but had been in the wrong place at the wrong time. Mr. Adair hadn't seen it that way; he'd very much seen it as the right place at the right time.

You have a habit of saving damsels in distress.

It was, he supposed, ironic for a man who liked men. Many had nothing to do with women, or they derided them. Not Alastair, who was often roused by matters of injustice. If they had possessed the same rights and respect as men, neither Alice nor Muriel would have been in as much distress. Evie, too, would have benefitted from a more egalitarian world.

Alice had been in a shitty situation indeed. He'd been passing through a pub regularly used as a drop point and meeting place for the likes of him. When he heard a scuffle in one of the back rooms, being drawn to chaos, he went to investigate—only to see someone he didn't know terribly well goading a young, well-dressed woman in a deep blue dress. She'd apparently been dragged off for some kind of ransom, but his hazy acquaintance looked to do more than that, which he wouldn't stand for.

Not wanting to take the chance, and assuming the man he didn't know so well was up to nothing good, Alastair knocked him out with ease. Then he asked the woman who she was.

Possibly, he could have thought his course of action through a little better, but his ability to think things through had come with age.

Alice Adair, she'd said, furious and looking quite ready to hit him.

He'd blinked with surprise; after all, friends of his own had already targeted her family, though none of them had suggested making off with the daughter. Careful not to attract any attention in the evening streets thronged with people, he took her back to her home in New Town. She'd needed some convincing and he didn't blame her for her caution, but he did stress the need to hurry.

In retrospect, someone might have noticed him; someone might have remarked upon it to someone else. It wasn't impossible for Lucas to have pieced things together, but at the time, Alastair was reasonably convinced he'd succeeded in his stealth. It wasn't as though anyone had ever come after Evie later, or James, or... he shook his head as he meandered. Part of him was in Edinburgh years ago, the other part in Cromer now.

It *had* been hilarious to see the look on Lucas' face when he'd discovered the room in the Adairs' house, formerly cluttered with things to steal, was largely empty. And Alastair, always one for a good bit of theatricality, had gone along with his surprise. It hadn't been easy, precisely, to break and enter.

Not every wealthy person was careless, and he'd told this one of the planned burglary.

He'd need to explain all of this to Paul. If consequences of past actions had finally come knocking, he could see no way around Paul being involved. Hell, he already was—the crow on the door was some proof of that, and there were those damn visions to contend with.

A brief thought of simply murdering Lucas before he could get up to anything came to Alastair, but such an action would lead to its own complications. If somebody like Sykes couldn't be murdered without question, a visitor with a memorable accent would surely attract attention. He and Paul had worried, however fleetingly, about Sykes' death being linked to him. An even more suspicious death would cause more worry.

All the same, he felt a strong desire to eradicate any threat against Paul, though he couldn't be certain it held any logic.

As his thoughts ricocheted with possibilities, he sat heavily on the sand and watched the water. His feet had taken him to nearly the water's edge. It was rather cold, and some rain had started, but that didn't matter. Chuckling to himself, he tried to let physical sensations ground him. *At least you haven't got a dead bird with you this time.*

Even if he suspected rather than fully understood what was at hand, he needed to tread carefully: if the shadows of his past were stalking him, more might be at stake than he wanted to risk. In a way, he took comfort in how his heart had changed. Now, he felt he had a life he wished to protect rather than abandon.

7
____

"He still not back?"

Paul inhaled sharply and felt his expression might be able to eviscerate Benson, had Benson been a less unflappable man. "Don't you think if he was, he'd be down here with me?" He let the three glasses he held in his left hand clatter to the bar. Heedless of whether they would, they still settled upright. "We almost always close up together."

There were a handful of times they had not; this wasn't remotely the same. When he might be too tired, or Alastair might be too tired, and one memorable evening when the nastiest of colds had got the better of Paul for the first time since he was a child. Seeing how ill Paul was, Alastair insisted he just go to bed. The next morning, Paul toddled down the stairs to find things tidied and set away to varying degrees of success, but all lovingly so. But once he'd settled here, Alastair took to the rhythm of numerous and seemingly unending chores quite well.

"Lad, don't worry," said Benson, trying in his way to be

soothing. That was kind, given he had just explained he thought his own room in his brother's home might be bedeviled by ghosts. Unlike some, who might take comfort in the notion of life after death or be galvanized by the principles of spiritualism, Benson was apparently disturbed by the suggestion. Whether or not it was true, or he was simply a bit intoxicated, Paul still felt badly for him. "Your man is certainly bound to you."

Benson really had little reason to be benevolent, right this moment. Many men would not be, should they find themselves troubled by a potentially ghostly issue. Noting his tone and recognizing it as an attempt to be calming, Paul waited a moment before he spoke. "That's not the problem," he said. "That he's not letting me help him, is the problem."

Though he still wished to see Alastair in ways he clearly wasn't ready to be seen, there were now pragmatic reasons underlying his curiosity, all to do with safety and feeling secure in the place where he'd spent all of his life. Thinking about it, he asked, "Will you put more sigils up?" The last thing he wanted was for whoever had left the crow to come bursting in with worse.

On balance, fixing a crow to the door hadn't been strictly harmful toward The Queen Anne, so it wasn't as though Benson's charms had failed. Still, if it could be further discouraged, Paul was in support of what might help. Benson had infused the place with protective witchery, and did strengthen it from time to time. He and Paul had developed a rapport almost since the first night they had met, and of course it had been quickly established between them that Benson was of a magical persuasion. Apart from knowing he was what he called a witch-hunter, Paul knew only flashes about his life. Though he said he lived in Norwich with his brother and his brother's wife, he also spent enough time in Cromer for Paul to wonder if he actually split his days between places.

Several times, Paul had almost offered him a room. He might, still, particularly given these recent murmurs of his brother's home being haunted. But wherever Benson stayed while in Cromer, it seemed adequate for his purposes. He was also proud in a strange way, not that anything he did wasn't strange, and Paul didn't wish to offend him.

"Of course," said Benson, regarding him owlishly from his place by the dying fire. The armchair he presently occupied was normally taken by someone else, but after closing, he sometimes lingered before going wherever he went at night. Then, that particular chair became his favored perch.

Paul was midway to the kitchen with the glasses when Benson's question came after him.

"He told you about his wife, yet?"

No doubt Benson wanted to hear if he was startled and the glasses would clatter in his hand. Taking his time to reply, Paul only said when he was back in the taproom, "He has." Then, a flicker of anger came. "He told you, first?"

"Christ, no," said Benson. "I think if he had his way, nobody would know."

"Is there any point in asking how you knew about her?"

"None."

"Then why bring it up?"

"Well," said Benson, his head lolling against the back of the armchair, "it just seems like his past has caught up with him, is all. Is that why you want more sigils?"

"Sort of," said Paul, and after a pause, he decided to give

up tidying for now. He went to the side of Benson's armchair and eyed the embers in the hearth. He hadn't yet discussed the crow's implications with Benson, for he couldn't imagine it going well if anyone else overheard him.

This evening had been busy, reminiscent of the sort he'd handled under his parents' supervision. When Alastair had come the previous autumn, he hadn't been entirely sure he would see more such evenings. Customers were dwindling slightly. But they'd come back, and the nights now looked more like what he remembered, and boded better for business and longevity.

Benson looked up at him; he exhaled a bit. He knew he could speak his mind.

"I've had two visions, somebody stuck a crow to my door, and Alastair is finally telling me things about his life before... well, before me."

"Two?" Leave it to Benson not to pounce on the mention of a crow stuck to a door.

Paul nodded. "I can't help but think it's all connected."

"Anybody would. What've these visions told you?" Benson seemed to know what Paul was before Paul had so much as spoken a sentence about it to him.

He remembered the moment Benson revealed the knowledge with stark clarity, because it was also the moment when he'd stopped assuming Benson was mad. After that, he'd concluded Benson was not mad at all, merely on the edges of society, and endeavored to include him a little more.

Paul had passed him his beer, and he'd accepted it with a sly look, muttering his thanks to a seer for his beer. It'd been so quick Paul might've tried to convince himself that he imagined it, but from that point on, Benson made too many asides to him about being the witchy Apollyon. There had been no imagination involved. The funny man wearing silver rings inscribed with runes thought he was a witch, a seer.

He was correct, of course. So after Mother passed, since it was clear Benson was of a witchy persuasion himself and they were already friendly, Paul had asked him if he knew anybody who might place protections on The Queen Anne. Benson's answer was, simply: me.

A lingering bit of firewood that had collapsed around its edges popped; Paul didn't startle. "The first was a waking one —and it was Alastair's stepson talking with his father. His blood father. I stood in the corner of a room, watching." He ran the vision over in his mind, again, trying to recall smells, sounds, anything more than their conversation. There hadn't been much besides the talking. Sometimes premonitions were quite specific in that way: focused on one or two senses over favoring all of them. In this most recent case, his hearing and sight had been more important.

Impassive, Benson said, "And the second?"

"My wrists were bound." Paul endeavored to ignore the memory of too much weight, the frigid water pressing all around him. "My ankles, too." He breathed deeply, eyes on the glowing embers. "I assume someone had thrown me into the water; I was drowning."

And it had been him; he didn't think he was inhabiting someone else's body. This vision had been far more immersive than the prior. He could have clung to Alastair all night after it. He was surprised he'd fallen back to sleep, but supposed exhaustion won out against fear.

More sympathetic, Benson remarked, "I'm sure Alastair loved hearing about that one."

"He said he wasn't going to let me out of his sight." Paul looked over at Benson. Droll, he added, with a small motion at the emptied taproom, beyond the windows of which was a night patterned with rain, "You can see how that worked out."

He hadn't realized earlier, but he did feel slightly abandoned. Though he did not take Alastair's penchant for dashing around personally, it was difficult not to feel a little neglected after hearing him state something so adamant as all that. Perhaps if he'd never said it, Paul wouldn't have noticed a contradiction. Sometimes, loving Alastair was as paradoxical as holding sunlight. He'd learned that allowing for some distance was necessary, and it hadn't caused him much doubt until recently.

Despite both the conversation they'd had earlier and the adamant statement about watching him, Alastair was still out and wandering. *Old habits die hard.*

"I see how it's working out right now," said Benson, and he was remarkably gentle for someone who could be so perplexing, "but that has no bearing on how it *will* work out." He stretched his legs. "As I said, you're bound. Doesn't take any magic to see it at all."

What if he just doesn't come back, tonight?

The thought came an hour later when he was in bed alone. He watched the play of shadows on his ceiling; he hadn't drawn the curtains and clouds still shifted against the moon after the day's rain. He did not think Alastair would disappear, mostly that he might make himself scarce until whatever internal tempests he seemed to possess tired themselves out.

After several minutes of ruminating, a more sensible person might have been wary of hearing quiet footsteps outside the bedroom. But he wasn't sensible and besides that, he knew them; Alastair was allowing himself to be heard. One of his specialties was moving stealthily. He usually brought to mind some type of predatory cat who hailed from far away.

He appeared in the doorway presently, and Paul sat up, hoping he was frowning, yet knowing all he really exuded was dismay. Neither of them spoke. Apology was written on Alastair's face, or from what Paul could make out of it.

But even Alastair, often a man of charming babble, didn't say anything as he shed his boots and overcoat, letting the latter settle on the floor. Then he came to the bed, now moving soundlessly without any heavy soles under his feet. Paul snatched at the edge of his shirt, untucking it as he did, and wrested him down for a kiss. Talking might not solve many of their problems at the moment, even if they tried to talk in earnest. But he could intuit what else might help.

With a quiet huff, Alastair eased down and went to his knees on the bed, keeping their lips close all the while. Paul was happy to shift under the covers to allow him more room. This, he thought, could convey his feelings more effectively than any conversation. Alastair's lips and face were chilled, and crisp nighttime air was still on his skin.

He didn't smell like a pub—stale smoke and spirits—but just the sea, leading Paul to believe he'd probably been outdoors for hours. He wanted to ask if he'd eaten, if he'd rested, but he thought he already knew the answers to those questions. Likely not.

Besides, he didn't much care if Alastair had taken care of such basic physical needs at this precise second. The urge to satisfy others was much more intriguing, so he eased his mouth from Alastair's and trailed his lips on his jaw, then lower to his neck. They'd discovered quite early in their association that this was a favorite spot; Alastair bared it to him.

With relish, Paul kissed lightly, then bit delicately, pressing with his canine teeth. After a few seconds of that, he traced aged ink on the side of Alastair's throat with the tip of his tongue. It gave him no small feeling of power when Alastair groaned and the delighted, low sound coiled through the room.

"WHERE DID YOU GO?"

Alastair thought Paul had fallen asleep. They'd had twenty minutes of dead silence after they'd fucked, which was always a good thing from his perspective. It meant they'd been thorough. The lull didn't feel too loaded. Just sleepy, if anything.

He glanced down at the top of Paul's head and replied, "Walked all over the beach, then around."

"Must've gone all the way to Overstrand."

"No, although my feet do hurt now."

"Weren't you worried about..." Paul trailed off. Alastair recalled, somewhat ashamedly, that Paul didn't know who, or what, to ask about. He was just astute enough to know to ask something. "I don't know. Weren't you worried about being intercepted?"

Amused, for even though he wished Paul was a little less quick, he would not want him any other way, Alastair said, "By who?" He did expect Paul to say Mr. Lucas, and was not disappointed.

"That Mr. Lucas, I suppose, whoever the fuck he is." What there was in Paul's voice, Alastair couldn't discern properly. Envy, perhaps, or resentment.

Wishing to disabuse Paul of the notion that Lucas meant something important to him, he decided to begin there. "We did business together, years ago."

"Like we do business?"

"God, not at all." He couldn't keep the revulsion from his reply. Temperamentally, they had always tended to clash. In terms of attraction, Lucas had never been of interest to him. "But he was a contact I had, and we did manage a few little operations."

His tone warmer now, Paul said, "You don't have to be coy with me. You weren't always on the right side of the law."

Indeed, that was the case: both that he hadn't been, and Paul knew about it. Of everything, he was most open about his past incomes. He was still allusive. But Paul, ever an expert at reading between what was said and unsaid, did grasp the wider idea. His paramour was a petty criminal who'd smuggled and stolen, threatened and bribed, forged and brawled.

There was one factor, however, of which Paul remained totally ignorant. Adair's money and its interest. After all, because of it, Alastair had stepped back from the majority of his earlier pursuits.

With a deep sigh, he realized that, instead of Evie or James, Paul now faced the risk of possibly being used as leverage or bribery.

Paul asked, "All right?"

"I'll tell you about the man who left the love letter this morning." It might be the case that someone else had left the crow, but this felt unlikely. "I doubt anybody can overhear us, here."

"Beyond anyone sharing that wall behind the headboard, I shouldn't think so. The place is locked up tight, and Benson strengthened his sigils for me tonight after closing."

Guilt washed over Alastair. "I should've been here, too."

"You should've." Paul seemed to mean it as simply as that, with no lingering resentment. Alastair rather thought they'd exorcised any poor feelings through orgasms. "But Benson says they should protect against eavesdropping, though I've little confidence they're effective that way. I eavesdrop every chance I get and nothing bad seems to happen."

Guilt gave way to delight. He did enjoy how nosy Paul could be, so long as it wasn't pitched in his direction. Many a time Paul had relayed gossip in this bed, some of it Alastair would never have guessed. "Maybe he means malicious people can't do it. I wonder what happens to them when they try."

"Perhaps a gull shits on them?"

"Oh, no, that's no good—has to be something worse. A bird shitting on you is good luck in some cultures, remember?" He'd heard it once from a Russian, who assured him it wasn't a joke.

"Very well. Perhaps they're struck by falling masonry when they try to listen to what they shouldn't. Will you tell me more about Mr. Lucas, or am I just to be content with knowing that you were never lovers?"

At that, after a kiss to the top of his head, Alastair tried to tell him about every thread that had woven together up to now, all the ones that he could see within this moment. Paul listened attentively, and why wouldn't he; Alastair knew this was all information he'd been yearning to know.

Lucas was a compatriot in crime, someone he'd known peripherally for years, and who had approached him to help undertake small, local, but lucrative burglaries. He did become a friend, such as friends from that demographic were. Generally, the plan was to break in while a home's occupants were on holiday, which was something that worked quite well.

They had accomplished what they wanted a handful of times, and although the papers murmured about this new spate of thefts, nobody was caught. Lucas chose well. Alastair was reputed to be incredibly light on his feet, which was more important than being light of fingers, and devilishly clever besides that. Paul chuckled at both qualities' mentions, undoubtedly thinking of all the times Alastair had accidentally startled him. He did think Alastair was clever, too; he'd said so.

Alastair could never see exactly why. It often felt like he was just careening through life since he did so much on instinct. Even though he wasn't terribly proud of having kept the bulk of how he'd come across his money from Paul, he readied himself to be uncomfortable in this telling.

Paul had never asked about how he managed to be financially solvent, but Alastair wondered if he ought to have said months ago.

He couldn't point to why a man giving him more than what his daughter's ransom would have been worth felt shameful. In the end, he supposed it wasn't. But contrary to the adage about honor and thieves, he did have a bit of honor. It had felt odd to keep the boon to himself. He understood why Adair had stipulated secrecy. On the other hand, in the strictest sense, he had not gone back on his word to Lucas by allowing their party to burgle a house that was no longer a viable target.

He hadn't known exactly what Adair would do to repay him; he only knew for certain that he had to pretend to go forward with Lucas' original plan, or it would look suspicious.

When he spoke about James' birth, and that being around the same time he'd felt the need to help Alice Adair, Paul said, "I think it's very kind, what you did."

"What?" Idly, he stroked at Paul's hipbone.

"Stopped. Considered them instead of just you."

"Well, wait until what I say next. Kind? Maybe. I won't say I *didn't* think of the baby or of Evie." He still was unused to talking about them with Paul, and in the future, he didn't want to quite as much as he was in recent days. Once all of this had been settled, he assumed he wouldn't need to. "Alice's father gave me so much money for getting her away from her kidnapper, and I did... accidentally tell him that his house was a target." He cleared his throat. "When I gave Alice back to him."

Paul sighed, which he felt and heard, as wrapped up as Paul was in his arms. "How did you *accidentally* tell him?"

"Well, I hadn't meant to. Lucas and I had set it in motion, and telling on things like that is..." He smirked. "Not done."

"Others, not you, had planned to kidnap Alice, then?"

"Yes."

"Makes me glad my family was never so notorious."

"From what I overheard in that back room, she was nabbed by a couple of lads who wanted to try for a ransom.

The Adairs are extremely rich. Her father and grandfather were known for collecting obscenely expensive antiques."

"Just like you helped Muriel," said Paul. "You really have got a heart of gold under everything."

"Tell nobody." Alastair grinned. "What I hadn't known was how close she was to her father, and how relieved he was that I'd intercepted her." It had been raw emotion, too, not merely a father pleased his daughter hadn't been tainted. He didn't want scandal to follow her, which was part of his insistence upon secrecy. That had struck Alastair as more pragmatic than anything. Such a well-to-do family depended on its reputation. But Adair's biggest motivation was love for his daughter.

"He absolutely made good on a reward," Alastair said, "I just didn't know quite how he would do it."

When Alastair had seen the room devoid of family treasure, he had his answer as to what Adair had done. It made sense to him then, and it did now. To a member of the average public, the objects looked like they should be in a museum for their historical significance and perhaps not just for their monetary value. At that age, Alastair had never been to a museum, but some of his friends had.

The collection had been comprised of small statues, ceremonial plates, bracelets, things dating to the Vikings and earlier. All of it had been accrued by Adairs over the years. To scoundrels who made it their business to understand hard value, if not proper provenance, they were worth something material.

But receiving recompense through this course of action had been unsettling. It had come unexpectedly, even easily, compared to what he was used to doing for money. Still, many others might not see any ease in shepherding a frightened young woman safely back to her house.

Christ, I haven't really thought about this in years.

He knew himself well enough to understand that his ability to ignore or forget was prodigious. Sometimes it felt as though his mind was only ever in the now. Even as he had actively helped Muriel, he hadn't really thought back to helping Alice.

The two weren't connected within his mind, it seemed. And though he sent funds to James, he still didn't dwell upon her being the start of his financial security. He and Alice hadn't even spoken more than a few sentences in the hectic time they had spent together; he was simply the well-meaning stranger who got her to safety while one of her kidnappers was sprawled on a dirty floor.

"So you had to lie."

"I lied how I always lie." Wistful, Alastair kissed the top of his head again. He thought, irresistibly, about Evie's words to Benson. *Don't lie.* He might have been too late, anyway. "I just didn't tell the truth, and nobody asked me. Lucas and the couple of lads involved in the burglaries... they didn't know about the plan to ransom Alice, or that I'd ruined it. Word hadn't traveled just yet, I guess."

Gossip usually spread quickly in the demimonde, just as it could in the beau monde. He supposed it was something of a blessing that the people who had organized Alice's kidnapping were not his lot.

Sadly for the Adairs, they were notable and wealthy enough to be the target of multiple such gangs. Their tailors and modistes were the best, while the papers often remarked on some valuable artifact the family had acquired. It was clear they possessed money for whatever whims they wanted to indulge, including their tendency to collect antiques, and they didn't always take particular care with their security. Alice was reputedly headstrong, an original who often wandered about without a companion.

As he thought this all over, he knew Lucas could have learned of what he'd done. The kidnappers could well have said something that reached him, or he could have made the inference himself. Lucas was many things, but he did not lack wits of a sort.

Alastair wanted to believe Lucas had only just found out, and that had propelled him all the way to Cromer. But it was more likely he'd known almost all along, then simply waited to act for purposes all his own.

8

———

The Queen Anne still felt secure the next night; it might have been Benson's doing. One day, Paul would need to trap the bizarre fellow in a room and force him to say more about himself. Alcohol would be out of the question for such an undertaking; Benson drank like a fish, yet remained as closed as a clam.

He scurried up from the cellar to the taproom, too preoccupied with finishing for the night to contemplate whether Lucas and his compatriot were keeping a nefarious eye on things or not. The canary *was* remarkably unsettled and it'd taken longer than usual to coax it back into its cage this evening. If he was more superstitious, he might take some stock in its unrest. Truthfully, as a few days since the poor crow passed without incident, the more he wanted to believe there was little reason to worry.

He knew that couldn't be true; all his instincts told him it wasn't. More likely that anybody who meant Alastair ill was just biding their time. One didn't need to be steeped in urban underworlds to make the assumption, and he was thankful not to have experienced the poverty or insecurity that Alastair alluded to. In the end, he had to assume Alastair had seen and experienced terrible things, some due to the penury that had permeated his life.

It was very pretty to think the dead crow had meant nothing, even if they knew it meant something. Alastair agreed with Paul's instincts. He'd explained that morning how Lucas had either picked up the crow idea from some fairy story—and Paul knew fairy tales could be macabre—or a mentor. Lucas, apparently, had been known to leave them as menacing messages. It might not have been a frequent thing, Alastair said, but he'd done it. He'd even once left one for a hostler who'd given him the wrong shade of horse.

Recalling this, Paul chuckled a bit to himself, eyeing tables and setting chairs back into their correct places as he walked through the room. The mentorship suggestion had struck him as somewhat funny, as though someone could apprentice or serve under someone else and learn the minute details of crime. In, of course, the same manner as any other trade: instruction, discipline, and practice.

Then, once he'd stopped chuckling and let himself ponder the matter, he realized it was probably how the most successful criminals were made. He decided he did not wish to ask Alastair, who seemed relieved to have finally discussed his past properly, but was still less keen on rehashing the exact details of his escapades.

Pausing near the far window overlooking the street, he thought, *I don't know why.*

It wouldn't have changed his opinion of the man himself. Yet Paul could tell Alastair was surprised he didn't take more issue with, especially, James being left behind. And, in turn, the money that was going toward his upkeep. He imagined a similar shame was there for other deeds, as well.

Idly, he ran his hand against the cold windowpane, eyeing the empty street. Closing had gone smoothly tonight, but he suspected the sudden cool weather was to blame for how subdued everyone had been. Even Maeve had not managed to set anything alight, which was a sort of record.

"It's so quiet out there," said Alastair.

Paul glanced over his shoulder. He passed through the taproom with some pint glasses somebody had left near the foot of the stairs. His preternatural forest-like scent was stronger now than it had been recently. It led Paul to conjecture he was more comfortable having broken some of his own rules around keeping things to himself. Having nobody able to explain why, Paul was content not to know for sure.

Sometimes it was lonely being whatever he was; sometimes he wanted a mentor or a friend who was more similar. He'd just have to wait and see if fortune awarded him with one, but he was happy to have accepting friends and a lover who'd called his talents the sight before he even did. Benson knew about him, of course. Miss Garland did, too, because he'd once explained it to her halfway through a third pint. The pints had been spread out over about four hours of lazing and talking, the lazing being rare for him. But it was enough to loosen his tongue.

She, for her part, seemed to simply believe him, replying she had an aunt who had visions of things happening to friends and family. It had made him wonder if perhaps everyone might have some kind of predisposition like this, but many lost it. That had been easier to think when he was slightly inebriated. More likely, there'd been too much stigma heaped against it, even if the days of witch-burning were past, so nobody spoke about it until they were at ease.

He looked back at the stretch of inky sky he could see. "I sort of like it." Paul sighed and his breath left a little fog against the glass. Not as much as there could be come winter.

"I would, if I weren't half-waiting for some miscreant to come swaggering in here."

"Well, it wouldn't be the first time," said Paul. He still gazed outside, letting his eyes focus on nothing in particular.

"True," said Alastair, "but I don't think you'd like this one as much as me. Or I hope you wouldn't."

"I don't think I could anybody the way I like you." A thought came to Paul as he felt the chill leech further into his fingers. He said, since they were alone and nobody would overhear, "James didn't always know about his father, did he?"

Paul couldn't judge Alastair for what he had done. He was realistic enough to know Alastair was rather capricious and always recalcitrant, but he also knew, as much as Alastair was stubborn, he was equally sensitive. The choice spoke more of desperation than recklessness.

Still, Paul felt some sympathy for James. He had no personal experience with anything like this, but he'd heard customers talk of similar things a handful of times. Men mentioning their own bastards and saying they'd left the mother and child in the same breath. A couple of women revealing they'd left a baby with a relative in order to seek work elsewhere.

None of it was meant to be overheard, of course, but from an early age, Paul had been observant and his hearing was always good. The non-existent yet still fully present colors that could radiate from people used to draw him closer, too, back when he still hadn't understood quite what they were. He also hadn't learned ideas of politeness at that age. Proximity made eavesdropping even easier.

Experience told him those colors could mean high emotion, and in these cases, there was never anything less than that. Even among the men naming their children as bastards, there was a higher pitch of something besides relief. Anger, or nerves, or regret.

"Nah, I wrote him a letter about it. The last one I sent, actually. Evie didn't want to tell him. She was lucky he took after her more than Arthur."

That squared with what Paul had overheard James say. Wanly, he didn't waste breath explaining how a letter might be the singularly worst way to reveal such a secret to someone. Alastair sounded hangdog enough.

And from what Paul had seen in the vision, James did favor Arthur just a little, mostly in build. His coloring was different; his eyes were green, Arthur's weren't, and his skin was less pale than Arthur's. His hair had been almost totally hidden under a flat cap, so what color it was, Paul couldn't say.

"He..." Paul hesitated. "Seemed to favor him a little bit. At least in his mannerisms. Their builds, too."

He heard the grimace in Alastair's voice before he turned to see it on his face. "I know," said Alastair. "That happened as he got older. She never talked to me about it, probably because she knew what I'd say." He set the glasses down on top of the bar and bit at his lower lip, then trailed his tongue nervously at the edge of his lip, above the shadow of a beard. It had been some days since he'd shaved, Paul knew. "Neighbors knew—how could they not? Mostly, they were good about it."

"I'm sure they didn't want to upset you, either," said Paul, who was well aware he must have carried something of a reputation, much the same way The Queen Anne had one, and the Apollyon family had their rumors of being odd.

"There was that, too," he said, and the nervous expression eased into a grin. "Being a visible deviant did have its uses. But everyone who lived nearby, they liked Evie. Everyone liked Arthur."

"I'm sure some liked you, too," said Paul, who couldn't imagine anything else, "you're charming, and funny, and you're kind when you want to be." He came away from the window and went to him.

"Oh, they did. But I'm just saying, the good regard was for her and him, too. Nobody picked on our boy or told him things we hadn't."

Noting he said *our,* Paul's heart ached anew for him, while his mind said Alastair had simply made a choice he had to live with, and was living with. He seemed happy here, and perhaps he hadn't been happy before. The only person who could say was him. "He might've had suspicions. The older he got."

"I don't doubt it," said Alastair. "He's bright."

"I'm sorry."

"Why?"

"I don't think it was easy for you to run from him." The way he'd gone hadn't been ideal; it didn't belie any warmth, but Paul wasn't going to tell Alastair something he already knew. It was clear he understood why James would be so livid and hurt. He'd been left, after all, without warning, and all the resources or money in the world would not lessen the sting of abandonment.

Alastair's composure broke for a flash, first cracking with a wince before settling into a twisted sort of smile. "But it was. Easy. I wanted it more than anything, and then I did it."

Then Paul understood what was at the heart of his guilt. "I think it's possible for many things to be true at once." He paused and thought of how to phrase what he felt. "You can be the sort of person who left his son..." Alastair's eyebrows rose, partially hidden by the long hair that often settled out of being tied back. "But you can also feel guilty. Feel shame. I don't know if you should feel either. I think you had to go, or you would have flickered out."

He had overheard people sharing things they'd done, just as he'd seen others retreat into themselves because they were too dutiful. He had watched them huddle in the pub with their alcohol of choice, be it blue ruin or beer, and drink until their eyes looked less harried. He wouldn't have wanted that for Alastair, who was vivid and quick.

Alastair said, "I hadn't thought of that."

It took little prompting for Paul to take his hand. "Clearly not."

Alastair stroked at his palm. "Maybe I'll try to think a little better of myself."

"It's not a simple situation." Paul met his eyes and sighed, thinking both of Alastair being young when he'd married, and of his youth being less of an issue than a need to forge a new home away from his father's influence. Marrying young was common, and so was desperation to fling oneself toward marriage. But it seemed Alastair had been rather relentlessly driven to it.

There were so many questions he still wanted to ask. He knew he needed to pace himself, and choose wisely what he did ask, or Alastair would retreat into himself again. *You have a lifetime to ask them.* It was still somewhat difficult, if only because he was naturally curious and wished to know all he could. But he would endeavor to do so.

"Doesn't seem so simple at all. I agree." The comment, offered by a stranger's voice, was accompanied by the creak of the old floorboards between the foyer and the taproom. To Paul's unpracticed ear, the new speaker's inflection sounded like the few customers he'd had from Edinburgh, a little softer than the way Alastair spoke, but similar.

Alastair's head turned so quickly Paul was concerned he might have done himself some damage. Instead of relinquishing Alastair's hand, he gripped it with renewed vigor. Taking a breath, he looked at the newcomer, too, a slight man in neat clothes that could have marked him as any sort of ordinary tradesman. He didn't favor Alastair's washed blacks, instead bowing to more conventional tastes, and his leonine face smirked from under a battered Derby hat.

"Knew I should have locked the door sooner," said Paul, pleased his voice was level and normal. Whoever this was, and he could guess, Alastair was not comfortable with his presence. That alone would have told him all he needed to know, although there was really no mistaking that this was Lucas.

"Don't worry, landlord," said Lucas, or who he presumed was Lucas. "I'm not here to drink." The smirk blossomed into a somewhat sharp grin when his eyes met Alastair's. "Alastair, so good to see you. You look well."

"I can't quite say the same."

"Oh, hush, I won't be in your hair for long if you play nicely with me."

"You could have set a better tone by not leaving us a dead crow, Lucas."

Lucas appeared, for merely a second, fully confused. "I outgrew that *years* ago."

Paradoxical as it was, given Lucas' unannounced and ominous appearance, honesty was in his voice. Paul could detect no deceit in the words, and he looked uncertainly at Alastair.

If he didn't leave it, who the hell did?

"Fuck off," said Alastair.

"Cross my heart, old friend. I've been admiring the sea, not falling into old habits."

While he was relieved to see Lucas because it meant he finally *saw him* and did not just suspect or know he was nearby, there were few people he wanted to see less. Despite their differences in approach and bearing, he hadn't ever hated him, but at the moment, he was fiercely protective of Paul and it translated to something like hatred.

"Aren't there supposed to be two of them?" Paul, ever stalwart, said. Alastair might have kissed him for his boldness; there weren't many who'd deliver the words with such precise calmness under these circumstances. "Miss Garland said so."

"Ah," said Lucas, "I guess the tart preceded me here? It'd make sense that she'd know local landlords." While it wasn't said with much spite, and Alastair knew Lucas didn't disparage anybody their work, something about the studied carelessness in *tart* irked him. "Yes." Lucas tilted his chin toward Paul. "There are two of us. Torquil shall be 'round later. I might've chosen my help better, but he's not so bad for a little errand like this. It's been lovely here, these last few days."

Gently, for Paul's grip was too tight, Alastair took back his hand. He had no gun and no knife, not that a knife would be much help at this range. But he wanted both hands free. Lucas' eyes flickered with interest at the movement. "I really am happy for you, you know." He came further into the taproom and sat in an armchair across from the bar, arranging himself in it with his legs over one of the arms.

"What?"

"Never mind," Lucas said. "That's not why I'm here."

Crossing his arms, Alastair said, "Care to say why? I don't want to talk all night. Though it's wonderful you've come all this way to see me."

"You owe me."

"I don't owe you shit."

"You do, and I'm collecting with interest."

Rather than sit, Alastair came several paces closer and stood next to one of the wooden tables nearest the armchair. He placed his right hand palm down on the tabletop, both to ground himself and appear less on edge than he was. "Can't do that unless I owe you, and I don't."

"You always were good at lying." Lucas grinned at him, devoid of affability. "The Adair house. The one we couldn't actually rob, because there wasn't anything in the fucking place."

"What about it?"

"Soon after that, I remember you just stopped participating, let's say."

"I had a family to think about."

"Yet no trade to fall back on. You were just a rat like the rest of us, yet you could somehow afford to leave the life."

"Got lucky."

"You did—because that sentimental, rich old bastard was so pleased you saved his daughter from ruin, he paid your way to leaving."

Alastair tried not to look too impacted by the words. But he didn't bother denying them. "How did you know?" He might've also asked when, but one would bring the other.

"Oh, a little bird told me you knocked him out. When he came to, she was gone. He said he would've gotten a right large amount of money for that Alice. We all gossip worse than fishwives; I don't know how you thought I wouldn't have found out." Lucas eyed him. Alastair hoped he hadn't gone pale. It was hard with his complexion, but not outside the realm of possibility. He felt a little like he needed to cast up his accounts directly on the table.

"I thought, at the time, it was a little funny you'd bothered to rescue her. Didn't strike me as odd, really, because you're odd. Just silly." Lucas shrugged from his casual position in the old armchair. "But when we got into Adair's house and *nothing* we'd schemed to take was there, I did start to wonder..."

"What the fuck did you wonder, then?"

"Did something tumble out of your mouth when you delivered the girl back home?"

If Alastair had been pale a moment before, he might be flushing now. He had felt guilty in multiple ways while looking Adair in the eye and chivvying Alice toward him. Telling the truth came naturally in that moment. Nonetheless, it still went against the dictates of criminality to cross a compatriot.

He was cut from different cloth than Lucas, though perhaps he hadn't understood how different until that precise juncture.

Like they discussed a dinner menu, Lucas said, "I can see by your face I'm right, and I already know I'm right. So don't bother making excuses. The old man sold all those trinkets and gave *you* all the proceeds."

Shutting his mouth before opening it again, Alastair asked, "Why now?"

"The hell do you mean?"

"Why not corner me years ago? You knew where I lived, you knew my wife and my son."

"Your son." Lucas chortled with mild derision. Alastair let him. "To be perfectly honest, I was waiting until it would cause you the most trouble. I didn't even know if *now* would, so I've hung about to make sure." He looked over Alastair's shoulder to where Paul still stood, silent as a shadow, and smiled grimly. "I think this will cause you more aggravation. I didn't think involving Evie or James would, though that did cross my mind at first. Her, perhaps, but... did you ever love him?"

Paul didn't stay silent after that, though Alastair half-wished he would. "What *else* has happened to make you come now?"

"Hm?" Lucas' eyebrows rose a bit, and he said more to Alastair than Paul, "He's quick, isn't he?"

Alastair couldn't muster a response; he was too awash with wrath at the question's sly, mocking tone.

"I've come across an opportunity," Lucas said, after a moment, "that happens to be quite nearby."

Tiredly, Alastair said, "I could just say no. I'm not in that line of work anymore."

"Of course you could, but I have a few things in mind to coax you into saying yes. Possibly, the most extreme one would be killing him..." Lucas nodded at Paul. "Which would take some work on my part and might end up rendering you useless with grief. But I'm not above murder." He added, almost apologetically, "I'm hoping it doesn't come to that, so let's just talk in the morning. Have you any rooms?"

Paul's unspoken indignation was almost palpable to Alastair, who stayed him with the merest, smallest raise of his left hand. Even if Alastair didn't want Lucas under this roof, either, it was obvious that Lucas wished to show he knew where to apply pressure to get what he wanted.

Well, Alastair could play at that game, too. "We do," he said, tempering it with a smile that wasn't true at all.

"Perfect," Lucas replied. "I'll deduct the cost of the room from my planned collections."

If there had been a weapon nearby, Alastair would've gladly used it to its fullest extent. Whether Benson's charms would prevent this, he couldn't say. He trusted they would, and it meant Lucas couldn't hurt them, either, at present. But had that magic not existed, hanging for murder seemed like quite a small thing if Paul's life, and therefore his own, was already on the line.

9

———

The prior evening felt like a fever dream. This morning, he felt a prisoner in his own pub. His eyelids heavy, Paul had accepted his usual bread delivery without any interest or zeal, prompting good Mr. Allen to ask with concern in his rheumy hazel eyes, "Are you feeling quite the thing?"

"Oh," he said, lying with the first thing that came to mind, "I might have a cold, but it's nothing too terrible." Forcing a friendly smile with closed lips, he said, "This looks lovely, thank you."

When Mr. Allen turned away to continue his other deliveries, he took the bread inside and attempted not to be too tense as he stored it away. But it was difficult to be at ease knowing Lucas was upstairs. Even having Alastair in the bed next to him hadn't brought its usual sense of peace, or of home, and they'd been restless for the few hours they'd managed to stay in bed. Not in any fun manner, either.

These early hours, normally soothing, were charged and heavy.

"If I hadn't sworn off romance," came Lucas' voice from within the otherwise empty kitchen, "I think I could like you. It's usually women for me, but I don't blame Alastair for settling down with you."

Though he jumped a little, he wouldn't give Lucas the satisfaction of whipping about to look at him. He was surprised Lucas was awake, as it was still early. But he also didn't know what hours thieves kept, apart from knowing the habits of one specific thief. Presumably, they varied depending on whatever things were being planned.

"Am I supposed to be charmed?" Paul pushed some canned broad beans to the side of a shelf, more for something to do than because he needed to move them.

"I would expect that because I've threatened your life, there's likely no way to charm you."

"You're smarter than you look, then." He put some canned tomatoes in front of the broad beans and eyed a tin of salmon. He knew he was likely going to confuse things for Molly and the cook when it came time to make meals, but he'd explain things to them later.

"Aren't you afraid?"

"Of being murdered?"

When he truly thought about it, he wasn't. It might be a false serenity, and he supposed Lucas could tie him up and chuck him into deep water. Cromer was obviously next to quite a lot of it. But practically speaking, Lucas had been correct: murder would take effort. That alone quelled Paul's nerves somewhat. One couldn't know precisely how one would react to the threat of murder until it existed, and he was rather heartened that he wasn't given to hysterics.

On the other hand, not everyone was a seer. He wanted to

trust, at least a bit, that the universe, or God—whom he didn't entirely believe in—or fate would show him how he died. So far, he'd only had that terrible vision of drowning, and as disturbing as it was, he wasn't sure it would actually happen. At times, he might just be shown possibilities, and he held out hope in spite of his fear that this was one such time.

"I've killed before," said Lucas, and his slightly perplexed tone made it seem like he was trying to understand how Paul could be so calm, "but it's more trouble than it's worth, oftentimes."

"So you don't actually want to kill me." Moving preserved vegetables around was a ruse that could only occupy him for a little while, so he turned to face Lucas.

"If you want the truth, no." Paul wondered why he would say it so easily, but Lucas answered his unspoken question. "I *would* do it."

Paul did not doubt he was capable. In even cloudy, autumnal morning light, he saw Lucas' face bore telltale signs of a rough life. His nose wasn't straight in a way that suggested it had been broken, probably more than once. A small scar rested to the left of his mouth, running diagonally toward his cheek. Paul had no doubt there were more scars in places Lucas would never bare to him. Alastair had them, all the result of rows and brawls. His were just often obscured by ink, in which case Paul could more feel than see them.

"I believe you."

"Good man. I just want justice for what he got that we didn't."

Perhaps you should have helped a girl, too.

"And you're a motivation he's never had, not as long as I've known him. You're just unlucky." It might have been as close to an apology as Paul would get from such a man, not that he expected Lucas to apologize for threatening him and taking up space in his public house.

The knowledge that Lucas had known Alastair for years blazed in Paul's mind, the envy following like smoke after a fire. "You think he wouldn't have yielded to you for his son's sake?"

Slowly, Lucas shook his head. His Derby hat must have been in his room. Today, his head was uncovered and revealed thick, ginger hair, cut short and going slightly to white at the temples. "I think he would now, even just having spoken to him last night. Make no mistake, I shall tell him James could be collateral damage if he decides not to cooperate. I have people who will take care of it if I tell them to." Paul opened his mouth to speak, but Lucas added, "Back then, though, when James was only a bairn? I never saw the love in his eyes that he has for you."

He knew he should be uncomfortable with the assertion. It seemed wrong not to love one's child as much, no matter the circumstances—and James' were rather convoluted. He wasn't. It probably made him cold, or Alastair cold, or signified something unsavory and selfish about both their characters. He didn't much care.

"Are you so good at reading people, then?"

"Part of the trade," said Lucas. "If you survive long enough, you become better at seeing what people value. What they fear." He ran a hand through his fading reddish hair. "Can't say what *you* fear, just yet, but give me time. I *have* heard you're a witch, that you're uncanny."

Dryly, Paul said, "What if it's bad luck to murder me, then? I could curse you with my last breath." He wondered if one of his ancestors might curse Lucas in the event he was murdered. Family tradition held that at least one or two were sea witches, although it was not the sort of thing anybody could confirm.

"I thought 'witch' might be some silly reference to how you don't prefer women," said Lucas, but he did seem to appreciate Paul's sarcasm. His eyes crinkled at the corners, somewhat, as though he might smile. "But it does feel like the air before a storm in here, so maybe it's not a euphemism."

Whenever the topic arose, and it usually did when alcohol was involved, Paul had found most people were remarkably open to the preternatural. His grandfather and father said not to tell anybody what he could do, but that had been said at a time when Paul was still going to school. Arguably, he needed to make friends, and children were so easily scared.

Little did his family understand how introverted Paul was, and how overwhelmed he became by ordinary things, like loud environments or being startled. If he didn't make many friends as a boy, it wasn't because he spoke about anything eerie. Since childhood, he'd grown out of the sense of overwhelm, but he still was a quiet man unless somebody was close to him.

There wasn't any harm in telling Lucas he had heard truth, not lies. "My family has been here for years, and we're often considered odd. You don't have bad information. I expect everyone knows my preferences, anyway. They're just too kind to report me," said Paul, cocking his head as he surveyed Lucas, "though *you* could."

In some respects, Paul liked that Lucas' minutely surprised expression implied he hadn't thought of blackmail. Perhaps there was honor among thieves, after all, and he wouldn't dream of divulging such personal information. About Alastair, at least.

In other respects, Paul wondered if he'd just handed the hangman his own noose.

"Why don't we see how we get on without doing that?" Lucas said, after several moments of charged silence passed. "I've never been concerned with who fucks who. Not if everyone's willing, and nobody's a child."

"Heartwarming."

Seemingly uninterested in proceeding any more down this line of conversation, Lucas said, "What do you have for breakfast around here? I want to be fed before I put Alastair out of his misery and tell him what's underfoot."

"*He* usually has something I won't share with just anyone." Alastair spoke from the doorway.

Try as he might, Paul couldn't banish a smirk from his face. "That's true, not that I would admit it to genteel company."

"Though I'm sure it's quite the delicacy, I'll be happy with toast," said Lucas.

"Let's go out to the taproom." Paul turned slightly to meet Alastair's eyes. "Molly will be in soon, and I wouldn't want to be in her way."

"She'll burn the toast if I'm here."

"You did always have that effect upon women," Lucas said. Paul returned his attention to the interloper.

"Aye, I frighten them."

"Oh, no, not because of that. What a pity you don't want them." Again, the barest start of a smile was on Lucas' face, and although Paul would never trust him, he did not have the sense that this was the most cruel of men. In another life, he might be a customer, perhaps a little rough or callow, yet nothing out of the ordinary. But men like this could be pushed into things they did not precisely wish to do, whether by another person or their own minds.

On a sigh that did little to release any of his tension, Paul led them out of the kitchen, passing a hair's width from Alastair as he went.

By the time Molly had arrived and was able to bring them a modest breakfast of tea and toast, their meager conversation was trivial and almost jovial. They had settled at a table in the presently vacant taproom. Apparently neither Lucas nor Alastair wanted to sit with his back to the door leading to the entry, so they sat next to each other, leaving Paul directly across from them.

It didn't matter to him if he faced a door or not; Alastair seemed ready to fell any more threats that might arrive.

He also trusted Benson's witchery, not that he was about to tell Lucas about its presence. "Well," he said, brushing crumbs from his fingers to the top of his brown trousers and eyeing Lucas, "now that we have fed you, why not tell us what —exactly—you want?"

Sipping some of his tea before he said anything, Lucas shrugged. "It won't prove difficult for either of you." He glanced at Alastair. "You've stolen things from houses nobody else would dare try to break into, and you..." he turned his head and regarded Paul. "You're local. You might prove helpful."

Blinking and trying not to appear too irked at Lucas' smug and dismissive words, Paul merely stared at him.

"Housebreaking is of no interest to me," said Alastair. "Been years since I've done anything of the sort."

"This farmhouse is supposed to be abandoned. It'll be easy for the likes of you." Lucas grinned, and Paul did not like it at all. "We're after what's under it."

"*We* are not after anything," Alastair said, through a bite of toast.

"What's under it?" Paul asked. He was too curious not to ask, though his annoyance was stronger than his curiosity.

"Gold, I reckon."

"And there wasn't any place closer to Edinburgh where you could find any?" Alastair's voice was laced with skepticism. Lucas ignored him.

He said to Paul, "I'm sure you've heard of a place called Trunch."

Reluctant as he was to admit it, the nearby village might be one of the few places where smugglers' valuables could be. "Yes." It was not especially likely, but of all the locations Lucas could have mentioned, it made a little sense given what he knew.

"I've been told I can become a fairly wealthy man if I go," said Lucas. "To retrieve what some poor fuckers couldn't retrieve for themselves."

There were tales, and Paul had grown up hearing them, of revenue men capturing smugglers before they could enjoy the spoils of their trade. "Just so I have it correct, your plan is to go to some abandoned house near Trunch and hope there's lost loot under it. Because it used to be a..." He looked at Alastair, who favored him with a bit of warmth before his face settled into a hard expression. "Drop point?"

"I'm given to believe it's true, if obscure. But the obscurity would've protected it." Lucas shrugged. "I've considered it enough to decide it's worth my while."

Crossing his arms, which Paul knew were muscled even under the long, dark sleeves of his work shirt, Alastair said, "Why bother? Who the fuck are you getting this from?"

Both questions Paul wanted answers to. He waited. Nothing about their guest said he was particularly sensible, and even though his enthusiasm was in evidence, his logic did not feel sound. "You know better than to ask."

Paul inferred that meant it was bad practice to enquire, a guess that was bolstered when Alastair huffed but ultimately held his tongue. He had little doubt Alastair would try asking again, perhaps not now, but soon.

Once he seemed to be satisfied that Alastair was not going to argue, Lucas said, "Now, I do think we shall have to plan a little bit before we set off. Torquil and I have maps, of course, but those are no match to acumen..." he met Alastair's eyes. "And local knowledge." He glanced at Paul.

"This has to be the most absurd thing you've ever brought to me," said Alastair. "But if I help, you'll go away."

"Yes."

And to Paul, who was only a novice in matters such as this, it seemed very much like Lucas might still be satisfied if there were no hidden money—as long as he managed to cause disquiet and trouble for Alastair in the quest to procure it.

It was clear that he felt cheated by someone who'd only stumbled into doing the right thing for a kidnapped young woman. Paul could not help but wonder if, under all Lucas' cavalier banter and snide little remarks, he was quite jealous of his former friend and compatriot.

"I can't fucking believe him." Alastair was almost snarling. He knew his anger unsettled Paul, judging by the concern in his eyes, but he couldn't help it. A couple of hours had passed since breakfast, and time had not served to mellow his feelings. "Such a petty, conniving little—"

"Are you certain he's gone out?"

"Saw him cross the road three minutes ago. I was looking out the window. He's out, and that other one—Torquil. He's out, too. He went somewhere just as Molly was dusting on the stairs. I heard her squeak when he walked by her."

"Right, then," said Paul, his shoulders hitched at least an inch above where they normally were, "carry on, I suppose."

Seeing how he held himself, Alastair tried to soften his tone, his words. "You could go—you could go visit Muriel. Just get out of the way until I help him."

"No," said Paul. "I'm staying; I'm not about to be run off by some newcomer who heard he could *get rich* off lost loot stuffed under an old farm near Trunch. That type of smuggling hasn't really gone on for years. I'd be more amenable if he wanted you to break into the lord mayor's house in Norwich. That would make more sense, at least."

There was little Alastair could say in rebuttal; he agreed. He was still stunned everything had come together so well as to let Lucas carry out this revenge.

Could be divine punishment for leaving James. As soon as the thought entered his head, he tried to disregard it.

While he believed in something like fate or fortune, the idea of a god who dispensed reward and punishment according to what people had done didn't square with his sense of the world. He'd known too many disgusting people who never paid for what they'd done, and too many wonderful ones who never saw anything good come of kindness. He'd seen nearly beatific people die too soon, and utter scum live to a ripe age. For his circles, a ripe age could be far less than that of more affluent ones.

Still, ripe enough for people on the street and near to the gutter.

"I know."

He sat on a small sofa in Paul's first-floor parlor—their parlor, now—trying to breathe normally and infuse his body with a sense of composure. The landlord's flat at the top of The Queen Anne was inviting, but sometimes it felt too small, so Paul had recently decided to remake a back room on the first floor into a space where they could linger. It had a view of the water, much like the upstairs flat.

It did share walls with two bedrooms. They just kept their voices down and hadn't engaged in anything lascivious. Nobody save them really used it, but Alastair had suspicions that Benson sometimes snuck back here and smoked his infernal pipe. The little space often smelled of the substance in said pipe and it was not tobacco.

Alastair huffed. Everything Lucas said had been unexpected, although not the means by which he had sought out Alastair, which he'd done with efficiency. After Paul had quit the taproom to answer one of Molly's questions about the kitchen, Lucas related how he'd managed. Not without a bit of relish, too, and Alastair wasn't startled.

Given what Benson had told him in The Bell, it all followed. Lucas had gone to Arthur, asking where Alastair had gone since he wasn't in his house any longer.

Arthur, suspicious, said he wasn't sure.

James, less suspicious, or more eager to send an unsavory looking man with a scar on his face in his adoptive father's direction, said he was in Cromer. The letters and their post-marks, of course, confirmed where he was.

It might've been folly. Perhaps for men who hadn't had his past, it would have been without risk. He had not thought of obscuring where he lived; part of him even hoped James might actually reply to him. All of him understood why such replies might never come, but always, his heart carried a faint undertone of hope.

Lucas was right to an extent. Alastair had not possessed the capacity to love James without restraint, whereas he loved Paul deeply. He hadn't wanted to be like his father, and when he thought back to those days of trying to be a parent, that fear still came to the top of his head. Yet he wasn't like his father, as it happened. He'd been present and not intoxicated. He was quite good with a baby, as well, for he was able to get James to sleep when Evie couldn't.

Discreetly, he'd also let Arthur step in as much as was feasible. That was tricky, given nobody wanted to confuse the little lad and there were concerns at first about righteous gossips.

If it had been up to Alastair, he would have had Arthur move in with them, but such an arrangement would've been exposed sooner or later. They could finesse dubious parentage using politeness, but two men living with one married woman would've set tongues going more than they were. Given Arthur was neither Evie nor Alastair's relative by blood or marriage, they would have needed to say he was a lodger.

Overall, James wouldn't have been as effective leverage as Paul was.

Alastair wasn't sure he would be now, except for the guilt festering away within him. Though he would never revel in James' death, and he'd do almost anything he could to keep him safe, he knew he'd do more for Paul. This, he was sure, made him a bad person. It was strange to feel he finally understood what deep love was like after years of secretly yearning for it. As though he'd been sleepwalking through life and abruptly woken at a cliff's edge.

"If that old gold is where he says it is, I would be surprised," said Paul. "It's not there, I'd bet."

"I'll trust you on that."

"I used to spend more time around there before my parents died. Near Trunch." Then Paul seemed to think better of elaborating upon precisely why. He closed his mouth.

Alastair saw an opportunity to lighten the moment. "Had a lover, did you?" He tongued the edge of his lower lip, looking up at Paul, who still paced a little restlessly near the sofa.

"Yes, well," Paul said, "I had someone whose bed I shared a few times before he got bored of me."

Immediately, Alastair went from smirking to frowning. "He what?"

"It wasn't bad; he just... he moved on." Paul shook his head. "I wasn't in love with him."

Sitting back on the sofa, Alastair tried to assess if he was being truthful. It didn't matter much, for Paul didn't seem too overset, just adorably flustered. "I see. I had lots of those *wasn't in love with him* types, myself. So this boy meant you hung around the area."

"I'm familiar with it. Edward and I used to walk around rather a lot."

"I don't want to involve your brother in whatever mad thing is about to happen."

At last, Paul sat next to him. "He'd be awful at anything under the table, much less actual crime. He *blushed* when he found out what Miss Garland does for a living."

Smiling, Alastair silently noted he had the right brother for him, then. "Did this loot *ever* exist, do you think?" He knew Paul had loved fairy tales and adventure stories as a boy, and now nursed a fair interest in folklore and legends.

Of anyone, Paul might have taken notice of newspaper stories or tales about smugglers' loot left behind because they'd been caught and ultimately punished. That was Lucas' account, such as it was. Alastair had little doubt that if he hadn't absconded to Cromer, Lucas might never have heard of it. But since he was here, and it was within a region where there were smuggling operations decades before now, he supposed it might have merit.

According to Lucas, who had explained more over his toast's crust, a pair of cousins had hanged for the crime of robbing with the aim of trafficking goods. But they had managed to stash the proceeds away before suffering the consequences. They hadn't told any authorities the real location, yet *someone* knew, someone on the inside.

As far as vague stories like this went, Alastair had heard worse. If it were true, Lucas stood to gain. Truthfully, Alastair was rather thankful Lucas hadn't decided to extort him for the rest of his life. It was as though he considered Adair's reward unreachable, or hadn't thought of demanding any small payments over time, and instead regarded Alastair as the means to an end now.

Or, thought Alastair, *he may think I've spent most of the money.* It was hard to divine the rationale of criminals, even if he had been one.

"It could have. Caches of old things, old gold, have been found in Norfolk. Ancient stuff, really," said Paul. "I also don't doubt smugglers left some of their spoils and they're lost. I've never heard of this specific thing. It depends on how credible his source was, doesn't it?"

"It may really come down to that."

He leaned his head against Alastair's shoulder. "Even credible people can get this sort of shit wrong. You know, someone's nan tells someone's father one thing, then that father tells their son something that's a little different from what Nan said... and so it goes."

"And there are no direct written records to really consult. Looters and thieves and smugglers..." Alastair fell silent. Though Paul knew him, he still felt odd if he directly referenced himself as any of those things.

"You're not going to write those things down, and I don't blame you."

"If we can write, anyway." In light of how little his father had cared about schooling, it was a minor miracle Alastair could.

"You can write."

"Mm," Alastair chuckled and slipped an arm around Paul's waist, "because my mother insisted I learn."

When this wasn't met with a wistful reply along the lines of, *I wish I could have met her*, for Paul had said it before, Alastair let the quiet be. There was, after all, much to think about.

But as Paul's muscles tensed under his hand, he glanced sidelong at him. "All right?" Even he had slid into asking the question, a rather Norfolk way of asking how someone was faring. If Benson was within earshot, he was mildly teased for it.

No reply.

Alastair gently, slightly distanced himself from Paul and peered at him more properly. His eyes were unfocused, but in an instant, Alastair knew they weren't precisely unseeing. Paul's waking visions didn't always look the same to him, though. The recent one in the corridor had seemed more like a grimace than anything else, like Paul was trying to subdue a particularly bad headache.

This one looked more like a fit, and he had the brief but unsettling thought that perhaps not everyone considered ill to the point of being locked away for it, *was* ill or mad. It disturbed him because he immediately thought of Paul locked away in some terrible place. Instead of letting his mind go to dark places, he kept his grip on Paul's waist and tallied his recent visions in his mind. It was his third. *They say things come in threes...*

10

———————

The room was dark and dank, and it felt underground. Entirely so, not like The Queen Anne's cellar, which had narrow windows allowing for the barest light. Here, Paul was certain he benefitted from some preternatural and false light, as there were no such tiny windows anywhere.

He looked to his left, then his right, and took an experimental step forward. The space was small, but not terribly claustrophobic. He could stand to his full height; he guessed a taller man might hit the top of his head. When he looked up, the ceilings were rough. The air hung thick and damp, and cobwebs dusted the corners, but he was able to see clearly.

His sense of inquisitiveness weighing more than his sense of unease, he leaned against a slight, natural outcropping in the nearest wall and waited. He hadn't the faintest notion what he waited for, or of where he was. When he was, either. The entire experience felt more lurid than life, as visions did, so he was confident the matter of when was as important as where.

It was nowhere he'd been, but a seer could travel through time and space in the abstract, not that he was precisely used to it. He wasn't sure if anyone would become accustomed to layers of meaning paired with a lack of context.

But he had learned since childhood that it did no good to panic—panic wouldn't lead him out any sooner. In fact, sometimes it seemed to make things all the more acute; alarm drew details and sensations far too strongly for his liking. He had a feeling this approach trickled into his everyday life, because more than one person had remarked upon his supposedly endless patience and calmness. It might not be the healthiest way to be, bottling things up, but it had helped him cope with possessing such a talent.

The first figure who came into the room made his heart leap from joy, not fear. Alastair strode in, as ever making a minimal amount of noise on the dirt floor. Paul kept still, not that it would matter if he went right up to him and touched his arm, his shoulder, or even his face. Touch was one sense that activated capriciously in these visions; he might feel cold water, and he might be able to have the earth feel solid under his feet. Beyond that, consistency wasn't something he could depend on.

"Mate, there's nothing here," said Alastair. He carried a squat candle in a cheap, thick brass holder. Someone behind him scuffled along, and Paul wasn't taken aback to see it was Lucas.

Then, as both of them stood right next to each other, they looked like they'd either fought or been in a fight. Alastair's lower lip was split, and Lucas' right cheek was bruised.

Interested, Paul rose and crept to Alastair until he was less than an arm's length away from him. No reaction, not that he expected one. He was as a ghost, or as a ghost was to him; Paul counted premonitions among his dubious talents, but hadn't ever seen a spirit. His own pub might be swarming with them, and he'd never know. Smiling despite himself, he reached out with a tentative pointer finger and grazed it against Alastair's lip.

He twitched, like he tried to evade a fly. Then he spoke again. "Sorry, but I think your man had bad information." Smugness roiled from him, and Paul had to chuckle. "Or he just got something wrong. That *can* happen—these old stories, you know."

"Or you just got here first," said Lucas, after a few moments of uttering garbled, angry noises that brought to mind an irate tomcat pronouncing its territory.

"How the fuck would I have done that?"

"You and that boy of yours," said Lucas. Paul assumed Lucas meant him. "You two could've managed something. He's uncanny, that one, and he's local. Has all sorts of knowledge, I'd bet, and this damn village has more than one cellar—"

"Careful what you say next." The meager candlelight burnished Alastair's face and pooled in his brown eyes.

"You did it before." Lucas was insistent and began to pace the small area, glancing in the uneven corners, seemingly convinced he might find the cache that he'd expected to find.

"I just did a good deed, and someone repaid me for it," Alastair said dismissively. "I didn't go out of my way to cheat you. Not then, not now."

"But that Apollyon," Lucas said. Pure protectiveness

bloomed on Alastair's face at the mention of Paul's surname, and Paul would have kissed him for it. "I trust him even less than I trust you."

"Why'd you even come all this way to exact your revenge, then? You seemed to trust me to help you with whatever the fuck this was supposed to be."

Going mulishly silent, Lucas scowled at him.

"You're not a child," said Alastair. "You should have known better. You just wanted to make my life a bit difficult, and you knew I was in Cromer, so when you heard anything to do with Norfolk... you jumped at the thought of dragging me into it."

"I would've come myself," said Lucas. "With Torquil. You being near, that was an added incentive to do it." But he spoke somewhat weakly. Even Paul could hear that he was trying to convince himself, and the idea of inconveniencing or scaring Alastair had been more attractive to him than money. Or, at least, it had been equally attractive.

He thought of Lucas waiting and watching, taking a little time to ascertain Alastair's life was worth disrupting before he actually did so. That wasn't the action of someone who *didn't* wish to cause at least a little emotional upheaval. It wasn't really how somebody interested only in money would behave.

There were probably a dozen simpler ways for Lucas to line his pockets, all of which had to be nearer to home for him. Despite what he said, he was drawn by the prospect of harming Alastair somehow. It was similar to any other grudge, with the difference being that they had each killed someone before. They were used to higher stakes than Paul.

Paul had never been able to get a straight answer out of

Alastair as to whether he had killed anybody; it just felt likely he had. He might not have done it out of bloodlust, but Paul would bet on him having killed in self-defense.

By comparison, most of the grudges the Apollyons had dealt with came by way of an incensed fellow landlord who was jealous of their latest ale, or maybe a chandler with whom they'd had to cut ties. Or from teetotalers more like the Mills family. In which case, the grudge was probably more for alcohol than a specific person.

This world of dead crows and lying and underground chambers was new to Paul, but it wasn't to either Lucas or Alastair. It made his heart feel bruised for the latter, who had, by his own admission, been a rather whimsical child before life set in and took that whimsy from him.

"This type of shit... it's all just stories. Somebody tells somebody who tells somebody." Alastair gazed around the room, then right through Paul, who still stood near to him. "*If there was anything here, it's been gone. For what it's worth, I didn't really think there'd be anything at all.*"

Lucas drew a small gun, a pistol, and levelled it at Alastair's midsection with a soft snick of metal on metal. Paul trusted Alastair was alert to the possibility, but it was still visceral to see someone like Lucas pointing a gun at him.

"You won't," he said mildly. "You'd get found out."

"You'd rot down here." Lucas stepped closer to Alastair, who stood his ground, looking at him with almost compassion.

"Mind the floor," he said quietly. The candle didn't even tremble in his hand. "It's not even."

"I think that's enough time to be under, angel."

Flinching, Paul said, partially aware he was coming back

to his own reality under enticement of Alastair, "You have to let me stay."

"I've never seen you gone that long."

"I..." Paul exhaled. "He was going to shoot you."

"Well, that does tend to happen amongst us awful types."

"You don't even know who I mean." Two strong hands were on his upper arms, petting him slowly. Disconcerted, he had to let them bring him back to where he'd been, where he was supposed to be.

"I think it's obvious who you mean," said Alastair. Gradually, he came back into proper focus and Paul gawked at him. "Who else could it be? And you've had like five fucking visions since all this started. I can't think it's coincidence."

"Three. That's just the third. Don't be silly," said Paul.

"Just? Your heartbeat's going like a rabbit's. I see it in your neck."

"Yes, because he had a gun pointed at you," Paul said, willing him to understand at least the urgency of that part. He lowered his voice, unsure if Lucas and his accomplice had returned to The Queen Anne yet. If they had, they probably wouldn't be able to hear anything said from here. All the same, he didn't want to risk it. "That shit he's looking for... it's not even there, where he's been told it is."

"Sometimes you see possibilities."

"Yes," said Paul. "Those feel more like riddles."

Even his taste of being tied up and sinking through cold water was, in essence, more of a preternatural riddle. He didn't know who'd done it, he didn't know why or how he'd gotten there, and although he did assume it was him, he could have seen it through someone else's eyes. He recognized the need to be wary, but that premonition wasn't as legible as what he'd seen between James and Arthur, or just now between Alastair and Lucas. "They're not full scenes, like this was."

Holding him, anchoring him in a way Paul had grown to depend on, Alastair took a few deep breaths and looked thoughtful. "Then we just do what I did before. We go along with it, and we don't tell him what you know."

"Is that wise?"

"Think he's a little too temperamental to just turn around and go back home because it's the practical thing to do."

THAT EVENING, the taproom lacked the cozy, calm air it had possessed the night before. No customers, regular or more casual, were particularly boisterous, but the feeling was more subliminal than that. Alastair wanted to mention that it was almost like the building sensed Paul was in trouble, or just harboring people he truly didn't like at his cost. He thought it was heartwarming that the actual establishment might want to look after Paul the same way Paul looked after it.

But to say any of this, he wanted to get Paul alone for just a moment. He couldn't shed Torquil, Lucas' compatriot in crime who had accompanied him down to Cromer on a frankly ludicrous revenge mission. Even if it was an actual attempt at accruing loot, Alastair could think of at least a dozen ways Lucas could have stayed in Edinburgh and made money.

Hell, he would rather have stopped sending James anything and paid Lucas off, but the possibility hadn't been brought up. It told Alastair that Lucas truly wasn't interested in material gain alone. If Lucas was motivated by money, it would have proved simple to pay him and send him on his way.

Unfortunately, Alastair had meant it when he'd told Paul that afternoon that Lucas wouldn't be swayed by anything practical, even knowledge of there being no treasure.

Besides, even if Lucas could be moved by reason, Alastair would not want to risk explaining—or obscuring—how Paul knew there was nothing to be found. At worst, if they relied upon the truth, Lucas was a superstitious character who might prefer trying to leverage the premonitions. No matter that they couldn't be harnessed on command.

"I've never been to England before," said Torquil. He sipped his pint, looking around the taproom as though it were some kind of menagerie and the occupants wild animals.

"It's underwhelming," said Alastair, though he didn't actually believe it to be so.

"I've found it lovely, so far," Torquil said, "but sometimes people can't understand me when I talk and I end up repeating myself. I was with a girl last night who didn't know what I said at all."

Alastair hadn't met Torquil before now, but he knew within a few minutes that the man was functionally Lucas' muscle. Short, but built like a pugilist, he was in truth friendly for someone who had so many scars on his hands. His fingers looked like they'd each been broken and poorly healed at least once.

"Imagine that." He hadn't encountered similar trouble himself, but Torquil seemed prone to mumbling. That might have posed most of the issue.

Cheerfully, Torquil said, "Still, I didn't have talking in mind, and neither did she, so it all worked out." It wasn't uttered with much lasciviousness or derision, for which Alastair was thankful. Then Torquil glanced up and saw Miss Garland enter the taproom with Benson, the two of them walking closely together and talking amongst themselves. "There's her friend. The one next to that man in the green, holding the glass of... gin, probably. Look at how he's swaying a bit as he walks, poor fucker."

Benson wore a moss green coat that had been dirtied and dulled over time, and might have started life as a formal morning coat. Whatever it had been, it was now a daily garment. As to him being a poor fucker, Alastair wouldn't necessarily agree. Benson seemed introspective and preoccupied with things other people couldn't notice, but not all that put out by it.

With an inward smile, he hoped either Benson or Miss Garland would make their way to his table, and perhaps distract Torquil. He didn't believe Lucas had told Torquil to mind him. He just got the sense that until the occasion called for force, Torquil enjoyed being amicable and it didn't particularly matter with who.

Lucas hadn't yet made an appearance this evening, which was all right by Alastair. Paul's shoulders were still much higher than they should have been on a normal night of trade, he noticed. He thought again of what Paul had seen, that Lucas was going to shoot him, and tried to decide how he felt about it.

That the man might try wasn't a shock. He didn't need a seer to tell him the possibility was there. It might have been present since they first met. Lucas was somewhat erratic. He spoke as though he'd had a bit of education or exposure to people with it, but his short temper hadn't been impacted by any book or moral learning.

There had always been some sense that Lucas wanted to be better than he was. Alastair wouldn't stake his life on it, but there had been flashes of uncertainty in Lucas' behavior. Cruelty toward the crows could not be excused as anything but what it was. Still, that he chose burglary as his trade and never went about it brutally did seem marked compared to what he could do otherwise.

For the moment, Alastair was content to tell himself that Paul also did see possibilities, things that might never come to pass at all. Paul could not puzzle out why, but he did say they felt rather different from things that happened.

His Paul was a marvel, yet also a riddle.

"Can we join you?" It might have been the most polished thing he'd heard Benson say.

Hurriedly, he nodded and made room for Benson on the bench he occupied. "I'd hoped to see you." Miss Garland sat on Benson's other side.

Torquil said to her, apropos of nothing except she'd just sat down, "Was your friend's name Amelia?"

"Yes," said Miss Garland, ever courteous. In her line of work, Alastair knew courtesy was essential even if one would rather glass somebody in the face, and Miss Garland was so good at appearing gracious that he never could tell what she actually thought. "She said you didn't try to barter with her, which I have to say, we appreciate."

Benson looked at Alastair. "Well, happy to oblige, lad." He winked. "Anyway, something told me The Queen Anne was the place to be."

Guesses could be made at what *something* was, though Alastair wasn't positive if it had more to do with ghosts, Benson's seeming restlessness, or witchery. Halloween loomed ever closer, and he'd never set much store by legends, but perhaps this year he should pay more attention. Until Paul, he hadn't a preternatural bone in his body. He loved the stories, loved listening to his mother tell them, and even wanted to believe something beyond the gray and dismal world he inhabited did exist.

The world beyond might be full of fairies and spirits and creatures who didn't have his best interests at heart, but it felt preferable to what he knew. In the end, he wondered if that childhood interest was meant to prepare him for life alongside a seer.

"I'm happy to see you," said Alastair, "in any event." Or, perhaps his childhood predilections were meant to prepare him for interactions with the seer's friend who talked to ghosts and bewitched pubs.

"I gather things are a bit... odd, here." Benson flicked his slightly red-rimmed gaze at Torquil, who was cheerfully nattering away at Miss Garland. Alastair suddenly suspected Benson had used her rather strategically to distract Torquil, but she didn't seem to mind.

"We've," Alastair began, choosing his words and his tone carefully. Torquil seemed jovial enough, but there was no need to tempt fate, "run into some complications."

"And you'll be going away for a bit."

"How could you possibly know that?" It was more rhetorical than in earnest. For all he knew, Benson had been talking to the spirit of his great-grandmother who wasn't confined by time or space, and she'd told him everything that was about to happen in the entire world.

The mechanics of the preternatural, and powers beyond what ordinary people knew, were baffling. It never seemed quite like science; there were inconsistencies and limitations. Paul having a spate of three visions—not five—was an example. Whatever tethered him to the witchcraft, or the magic, whatever one wanted to call it, seemed to be stimulated into action by Lucas' proximity. Similarly, Evie had supposedly come to Benson under the same compulsion.

Not supposedly. Alastair believed Benson. In short, everything seemed more connected than he'd ever been given to expect, and he couldn't tell how he felt about that when he was being called upon to unearth somebody's lost stash of loot. All because he'd helped some girl get back home to her father when he was too young, impulsive, and idealistic to think about the pragmatic implications of doing so.

Even if Adair had never offered him recompense, someone still could have tattled on him for liberating Alice, which may well have been regarded as a betrayal to fellow miscreants. Some of them were drawn to unsavory opportunities afforded by situations like kidnapping, as antithesis as it was to Alastair. They might have been disappointed in losing any chance to abuse Alice in some manner, and therefore angry with him. He should have considered it a little more closely. If he had, maybe he wouldn't be so caught off-guard now.

"The look on your face," said Benson, taking a drink of whatever gin he'd brought with him. The smell wasn't from The Queen Anne's favored gin, Alastair could tell that much even amidst all the somewhat nauseating scents within the taproom. Unwashed bodies, old wool, warm pipe tobacco, beer. "Is he going, too?"

Alastair followed his eyes to Paul, who was talking—looking almost normal, save for the set of his shoulders—to a regular customer called Rob who always seemed to have an air of nerves. "I can't imagine he'd be all right being left behind." Who would take care of the pub in that event, he couldn't say.

More pertinently than that, he didn't suppose Lucas would want his leverage to remain safely behind in Cromer where it could not be used to its greatest effect. And Torquil didn't appear the sort of accomplice who could be trusted to exact punishment against Paul without supervision. He lacked that self-directed air.

"Could close up for a few days and just trust the residents for a little while. You've got the money—he knows that, now."

It was like Benson could read his mind. *Maybe he can.*

"We could have you stay, too." He tilted his head a little and regarded Benson, who hadn't spoken much about the strange activities that had been happening at his brother's house since alluding to them about a fortnight ago. He wanted to ask, but would not, if the activity might be following Benson rather than remaining stuck on one location. He seemed skittish around the subject, but Alastair hadn't noticed any bizarre new happenings whenever Benson was around. Bottles flying off shelves or suchlike. "Why not?"

Lucas would be gone, as he would be going to Overstrand and Trunch on this stupid jaunt. That left the room he'd claimed open. Paul might have something to say about Benson running the taproom, but he wouldn't be if he were just staying and minding the place. Perhaps Miss Garland could stay too, if she wished it, and she would be a far better stand-in for Paul. She could deal well with the public, and even if she didn't want to serve any drinks to anyone, she might be persuaded to let rooms.

Sighing to himself, Alastair thought that could do quite nicely. He wouldn't want either of them to feel put upon, or for Miss Garland to feel unsafe somewhere she was staying on her own. But together, they would likely make a good team.

Alastair had not voiced that he didn't want Lucas to come back, whether it meant slipping something into his drink or maybe throttling him in some alleyway. It wasn't the sort of thing one discussed in either polite company or with one's lover. Largely, he was angry, which bred an imposing wish to ensure Lucas could never interfere with anything again.

He did not necessarily feel Lucas would be a threat after all of this had concluded, but he had made a nuisance of himself and that couldn't be forgiven. The fury might pass, Alastair knew. If he searched himself, he didn't wish to murder Lucas. All the same, his heart wanted to convince him that he and Paul would be better off if he did. Since he could not disregard it entirely, he tried to tell himself it was a somewhat noble desire, or at least the sort of thing that would ensure there were no loose threads.

Looking shrewd and a little too knowing, as though he'd read Alastair's mind again just then, Benson said, "Could do. It's a compliment to have his trust. And yours."

11

Paul was ashamed to admit it, but he had never thought about leaving The Queen Anne as an adult, mostly because he wasn't sure when he would be able to do so. The thought did unnerve him a little. More than a little, perhaps. One could hardly blame him, he thought, given the circumstances. It might not be just leaving the establishment that bothered him, so much as the person necessitating he did so. It wouldn't be a holiday; it would be a trip that might end in injury or worse.

He knew he was nervous when, at almost two in the morning, he was actually well and truly pissed from too much brandy, some exquisite French stuff that he couldn't be bothered to recall the name of while he sat on his parlor floor watching the fire. It bloomed on his tongue like honey did, but he liked even more how his limbs felt warm and relaxed.

Alastair had remarked down in the taproom how tense he'd looked. *Well, I'm not now.* Whenever he came back up, he'd see.

He'd closed up himself, then gently chivvied Paul to the

flat, urging him to relax and telling him everything would be all right. Lucas had told Alastair to come to his room after closing.

Paul believed Alastair's assertion that things would be well, but he did not have to like the evasiveness with which his new customers were operating. Sipping the brandy and focusing on one smoldering bit of wood, he concluded that was something he could contemplate more thoroughly whenever this matter with Lucas was sorted.

It was such a strange thing to have two criminals under his roof whom he didn't trust, but who weren't likely to strip the place of anything valuable. All the money was up here anyway, and that wouldn't deter anyone who was very serious about stealing. No, it was an obvious thing for unsavory men to want, and it was one reason why he knew Alastair was not equally unsavory now.

When he'd run inside last autumn, he'd sought safe harbor from a man who was angry at him, but not because he'd stolen or harmed. He'd helped somebody in love. Paul smiled to himself and leaned against the edge of the sofa, knowing it was a woeful thing to use to support his back.

"Fuck, I'd forgotten how much he can talk," said Alastair, and Paul watched his scuffed boots come through the door first. Alastair sat on the little bench they kept just near the entry to the landlord's flat, and made quick work of removing his boots. "And we're not friends. If we were, we're not now. No idea why he keeps talking so incessantly to me when it's clear I just want to come up and be with you."

He crept his way properly into the room, still speaking. "I guess the plan is to go Trunch the day after tomorrow. Now that he's got my cooperation, he doesn't seem to be in any special hurry." He lowered his voice and added, "Not that he knows what we know."

This seemed to be the moment he realized Paul was not seated anywhere he normally lounged when he was alone in the flat. He paused, both hands on his hips, and looked around.

"Down here," said Paul. It would have been obvious with a few more steps, but he also didn't want Alastair to collapse in a heap unless it was for distinctly carnal purposes. The lit fire was quite near, and what with the floors being so uneven due to the way the building had settled, things could go from comical to alarming too quickly with no room for carnal in between.

Sykes had died because he tripped, after all.

"I see," said Alastair, taking in the state of the brandy bottle and Paul's splayed legs in an instant. "How's that cognac treating you?"

"As you see," said Paul, offering him a smile. "Quite well. Care to join me?"

"I'll join you on the floor, but I don't think I should get so pissed."

Knowing there was no point in denying it, Paul sighed. "I'm not so bad. I might be all right come morning." He brightened when Alastair settled next to him.

"You will," said Alastair. "You seem lucid enough." He pressed a gentle kiss to Paul's forehead.

"What did you let your new boss decide?" Paul did resent being kept out of whatever sort of talks were going on. It seemed circular and pointless to him, for Lucas had to know Alastair was relaying most everything to Paul anyway. But someone had to mind the taproom and there was nobody better than its landlord.

Alastair narrowed his eyes in confusion, then seemed to realize who he meant. "He's not my boss, and he's not your boss, and he didn't decide anything." Paul stifled a chuckle. Alastair could be quite oppositional when he chose. "I want him gone as soon as possible. Out of our lives and well away from here. If that means going to Overstrand on a merry chase, so be it."

"Trunch, not Overstrand. And I'm coming too," said Paul. "If you think I'd let you get away with traveling by yourself with him and that oddly pleasant one, you're wrong." He swilled some brandy from the glass he still held, though he'd also been nipping from the bottle. It was rare that he had a drink in each hand for himself. Part of him knew he shouldn't be drunk at all while Lucas and Torquil were underfoot.

For his part, Alastair took the bottle and brought it carefully to his mouth. Paul was suffused with the urge to kiss him, seeing the lips of the bottle meet lips of flesh. But they'd discussed at least once the importance of sobriety when kissing or fucking.

It seemed hazy to him now, but he knew they'd addressed it in their early days. *Back when he woke on this sofa after a night of too much drink.* That felt near and far, then and now.

"I know," said Alastair, after a couple of slow, measured swallows. "Benson and I were talking about it downstairs."

He smiled; he had seen them at a table with both Miss Garland and Torquil, who were absorbed in conversation. Paul had seen enough genuine ones to know when someone was feigning, and Miss Garland was definitely feigning. To what end, he had not known. She hadn't been lacking in clients of late. Though she was welcome to prospect and screen in The Queen Anne, the customers there were very often regulars, most of whom were not able to pay her properly.

He usually tried to push interested visitors her way. Discreetly, of course. Although Grandfather, Father, and Mother had never openly discussed it with him, he reckoned it was just the landlord's lot to do so. Everybody had to make a living, and she wasn't hurting anybody.

"I can just close up for a couple of days. We've got Jack and Ned, as usual, but they have their own routines. I know they'll be all right." They were long-term lodgers who'd come during his mother's time as landlady, before he'd met Alastair. Both were trustworthy enough.

Then he realized he didn't know what the plan really was, past not telling Lucas there wasn't any loot where he thought it had been left all those years ago. "Or... what are we doing, again?"

"We'll go the day after tomorrow and try our luck," said Alastair, keeping his voice to barely a murmur, "well, he'll try his luck—the way he sees it, it'll be easy to get gold and old jewelry out of an old cellar under an abandoned house without catching anyone's attention. As he's heard it, it's a good cache, but nothing the four of us can't handle."

The light frown on Alastair's face made Paul trail fingers against his arm, stroking the muscle under old, soft wool. "What?"

"Something just feels off," he said, brushing some of his own hair behind his ear with his free left hand. "He seems eager; I don't think *he* is what's off. All of this just seems too convenient, doesn't it? Besides, if you're right, nothing is there. And this is a long way to come for a mediocre stash of gold…" Alastair fell quiet. "But I remember thinking almost any amount of money was a good amount. Until I had enough."

He looked sidelong at Paul, who as good as melted under the glance. "I could be right," Paul said, keeping his voice low, too. He had the vaguest notion that they should move on to some other vein of conversation. He set his empty glass upon the floor, careful to choose a patch of wood that was level. "So, we leave. I'll just shut up the taproom and keep the front locked the way I do at night. Jack and Ned have their keys."

In effect, they allowed entry through the main door, but weren't skeleton keys that could open any other important locks. Father had kept them on hand for the rare lodger who was also worth trusting.

"Benson said he would stay," said Alastair. "And I thought perhaps Miss Garland would be good at dealing with the public."

"Neither of them can serve alcohol, strictly speaking," said Paul, thinking it over. "But I'd not mind having them here." The idea of Benson being in the building gave him an odd sense of comfort. His charms worked, but it felt natural to assume they'd work even better with him in the public house. "Is he here, now?"

"I put him in the room next to Lucas'." The smile Alastair gave him then was almost demonic, and Paul had to lean forward and kiss him, if just briefly. "If there are any nefarious discussions, Benson will know. He's got hearing like a bat."

Wistfully, Paul said, "It's good to have friends."

"It is, angel, and none of us will let anything bad happen to you or your public house."

Paul gazed at him, wondering if he should say what he was thinking aloud, or if he should let it remain unsaid. Men who weren't known for their goodness were just rooms away, and the stairs up to his own flat were creaky enough that he was confident he'd hear almost anyone but Alastair approach. The second stair to the top was especially loud.

Likewise, the second set of stairs that lead to the back of the flat were well maintained but similarly prone to talking. The one time he had not registered someone's approach, he'd been transfixed by Alastair. It had only turned out to be Muriel coming to say goodbye to him because Alastair drunkenly told her when to meet him in Paul's flat the night before.

The same night he had been so drunk, he'd let himself into the flat and flopped on the sofa only to fall asleep. When Paul had found him the next morning, he was mildly convinced he was dreaming. He didn't know what else to think when a man with beautiful dark hair and graceful limbs that could still rip him apart was magically sprawled on the same sofa his parents had kept since he was a boy.

Things like that simply didn't happen to him. He could see the future, or parts of it, but it was something he couldn't direct, or count upon for delivering anything exciting. It had also been part of his life since childhood, which rendered it rather ordinary to him. For him, premonitions didn't feel preternatural. Alastair, however, did. He brought to mind fairies who weren't so devious. According to the tales, they nearly all were.

But in this case, the fairy loved Paul and seemed to

temper any of his own deviousness. Or perhaps Alastair was more like a creature who lived closer to the water. He had said he preferred to be close to the sea many times. A selkie, maybe, or a mermaid who was less maid, more man. Without being preternatural himself, Alastair roused every feeling Paul was supposed to have about witchery, his own included.

It was Alastair's turn to stroke his fingertip against Paul's arm, tapping him a bit. "What is it?"

He must have stared too long. In fairness, the little fire splashed them both with light, painting Alastair with bronze and marmalade tones that rendered him devastatingly pretty. Paul felt he had every reason to look, and reminisce, and lose his thoughts. Cogency be damned.

Under influence of that soft touch, it just came out. It was a mad hunch, but he'd learned to lean into what Alastair wasn't saying and divine more of the feelings he tried to repress. Being able to see colors around him helped, but it was even more intangible than those.

Paul found the truth in his lover's gestures and tenseness and minute expressions. "Are you going to kill him?"

IT DIDN'T SEEM wise to answer out loud. He didn't *want* to kill anybody, in truth, but he would do so if it meant protecting his present circumstances. Paul's ability to read him, never mind the future, was still a source of joy and mild terror. And in this case, he wasn't precisely afraid, but he was somewhat pleased Paul mentioned it so calmly. Granted, he was a little drunk, pleasantly so. He was, nonetheless, more lucid than most slightly pissed people could be.

Rather than speak it and risk being heard, however small that risk was, he brought a careful finger to the underside of Paul's chin and tipped it forward a little so they faced each other. With a very slight smile, he shrugged and nodded once. *Maybe.*

Whatever he expected to find in Paul's eyes in return, it wasn't satisfaction. But he should have known. When he'd relayed the news of Sykes' death, Paul was admirably pragmatic in response. This was even more personal than that had been.

Lucas had come into Paul's carefully ordered world and taken up space without recompense. It was a little strange compared to others, but Paul managed it all with aplomb and aptitude. Now, Lucas was instigating a wild little jaunt to a place where he thought treasure was, and it wasn't. He wondered if contact with certain people or events brought about more visions for Paul, like someone whose body couldn't tolerate a bee sting might reject it. *Or stop them from breathing.* He'd seen that once and it had been horrifying.

Deciding he didn't want to take the analogy any deeper, even within his own head, he said, "If that pleases you."

"It does," said Paul.

Like he was idly petting a cat, he stroked under Paul's chin. "You are always a little more feral than I expect you to be."

"Do you like it?"

"Love it." He answered honestly, for he couldn't imagine loving Paul with anything less than devoted fervor.

After an unbridled grin, Paul said, "Good. I want to keep you, so I'm glad you're not bored."

"Bored?" He hadn't realized that was a worry for Paul, but was happy to reassure him.

"Yes. I'm nobody. I've told you that before. I'm just a man with a pub that I've never left, just a..." Paul sighed. "A nobody."

Were it not for the seriousness with which Paul said it, Alastair might have chuckled at the vaguely perplexed expression on his face. He felt no derision, only amusement and pleasure at the thought of reassuring him. "Angel, *I'm* nobody. I've no ties to anything—no pub, no family business. I hate my surname; it just reminds me of my father. If you're a nobody, we can be nobodies together."

He relaxed the hand under Paul's chin and brought it back to his own side. Driven by a relentless need to wander about, he had also come here. But Paul had quelled that urge. The sense of needing to move, to do, had never left him. He supposed it wouldn't, that it was just part of him and it wasn't strictly bad. Yet Paul stilled him.

"That isn't so bad of a prospect."

"No."

Contented, in spite of all the complexities that had been introduced recently, Alastair watched the dying fire and let his eyes go unfocused. His mother had said there were witches who could divine things from flame or control it. He had never met one, unless he counted Maeve, who only seemed able to create and lose control of small amounts of fire.

"You know," said Paul, "if you wanted, you could always take my name."

"Are you asking me to marry you?"

Enamored with the suggestion, Alastair smiled, his eyes

still on the embers and little flickers of flame. He knew Paul had recognized quite early that he loved men. According to him, he had never bothered to try to sleep with women. As such, he'd probably rarely given thought to marriage proposals. But during one of their earliest conversations, he'd also let slip something about how he'd always wondered if a marriage between men was possible. It had been in the context of talking of Abigail and Muriel, who were ready to run away and marry in all but the legal or religious ways.

Paul had mentioned, in brief, wanting that possibility.

Well, he'd cut himself off from finishing the sentence, but Alastair could tell what he was saying from what he didn't say. Even at that early juncture, when he was amazed that a stranger gave him keys to his flat and trusted him enough to take his word on what he was trying to do for Muriel, he'd found Paul deeply intelligible.

"Well," said Paul, and Alastair felt him quiver with emotion. "It couldn't be real, if I was."

He pulled Paul almost all the way into his lap. "It would. Maybe more real."

"What do you mean? It wouldn't be the same as you and Evie being married." Alastair understood he meant literally, as in it wouldn't be binding or recognized. "Which, by the way, I'm a little envious of."

With abrupt clarity, he knew why Paul was a little drunk on his own floor rather late at night. A bevy of things had descended upon him, and not all of them had to do with Lucas and Torquil, or even what tomorrow might bring. Paul had, quite simply, learned about the man he spent his life with. He was getting a taste of the things that man had left behind. He now knew there'd been a wife, and a child, and—

It was enough to drive anybody to find succor through a bit of drink. On balance, Paul was handling things better than most men of Alastair's acquaintance would.

"You don't need to be," said Alastair, but he knew there might always be envy toward men whose loves were considered correct. He often felt it himself. "It was only to help both of us. Get us out of our parents' houses."

"No," said Paul, "I know. I think that's lovely, if you want the truth. I don't know if I could do the same for anyone. But you did. I've thought about it with Muriel—maybe I'd have married her to help. Her father approached my parents when she was about sixteen, and they had none of it."

"But?" It was obvious Paul didn't want to talk about Muriel, or what he might have done for her.

Moistening his lips with the edge of his tongue before he replied, Paul said, "It won't matter, us being together. You and me. When we're dead, no one will know what we were." He shook his head a little. "What we were won't be *anywhere*. Not on headstones, not in ledgers. And that makes me furious."

Rather unprepared for the weight of hearing it, Alastair hugged him closer. He'd never thought such a thing. Now he would. "But there are so many marriages that don't matter to the people in them," he said. "For all they're remembered and on the record."

"That's part of what makes me so angry. It's wasted on them, isn't it?"

"Suppose so."

"I'm sorry," said Paul. "None of this has anything to do with what we need to deal with now."

Alastair thought it did. He could see how things were connected, in any event. "You have nothing to be sorry for.

The man you want to marry brought chaos to your step. If anything, you should be turning me out on my ear."

"I couldn't. Even if I didn't love you, I've always wanted a bit of adventure."

"And I've always wanted a home."

Paul rested his head on Alastair's shoulder, and Alastair played lazily with the deep brown hair at the nape of his neck. "You probably wouldn't want to take Apollyon as your surname, anyway. Too much alliteration."

A laugh did escape him after he heard that. "We could still be married," said Alastair. To him, they already were.

"I don't know why I care," said Paul. "It all seems archaic when I think about what it means... ownership. Still, I want recognition. I love you. You love me. And we can't have *any* recognition or respect for it."

"Heart and head can be at odds, oftentimes," said Alastair, trying to calm him as best he could. "It doesn't make you weak if you want what can come so easily to others. The entire thing is just unfair." Archaic was an excellent word for it.

He knew with certain serenity what he was to Paul; it wasn't anything he'd been to Evie. There were similarities. He loved both of them. But there was no dutifulness to be found here, and what he'd done before was rooted in a duty of care, not any passion or interest. He was quite a different husband, a better husband—or perhaps a wife—to Paul Apollyon, for all that he couldn't take his name.

12

———

Feeling mildly ill while recovering from a little too much drink was not the way Paul wanted or expected to spend the day before he was supposed to make an incredibly awkward journey. He wanted to be optimistic, but it didn't come so naturally to him, and besides that, it felt beyond any definitions of optimism to hope any journey with Lucas, Torquil, and Alastair could be anything but tense.

At present, he thought Benson's sipping was too loud. He'd even had to leave the canary up in the flat. Neither reaction to what were, in reality, minor noises portended well for tomorrow. He would be recovered by then, but it had been a while since he'd drunk enough to have lingering effects. He wondered if his tolerance had changed; he didn't often partake.

"Are you quite finished?" he asked Benson. His hand paused over the ledger he was trying to annotate. He couldn't blame Benson for his peeved state, and certainly not for his slightly hungover state. But logic wasn't his strong suit at the moment.

Benson glanced at him from further down the bar. "Late night, was it?" He knew full well what was wrong.

"You could say so." The weather taunted him. It was agonizingly clear. Not warm, as it rarely was this time of year, but bright and almost lucid. He saw exactly how clean he kept his own business due to the quality of light streaming indoors, and felt a flash of pride. Of course, it wasn't just him who did. Molly and the others who worked for him had to be credited, too.

"It'll pass," said Benson, "or you could keep drinking, and then it won't matter."

"I want my wits about me."

"Wise." Benson put down his cup. A more predictable person would have filled it with tea or coffee, but he never did unless they were cut with something much stronger.

Hoping he didn't sound as though he wheedled or was nervous, Paul had to confirm Benson was feeling able to keep an eye on The Queen Anne while he and Alastair went to Trunch. "Are you positive you want to mind things for a day or two? Please don't open the taproom. I don't want to get in any trouble for that. You're welcome to drink whatever you wish, though. And there aren't any deliveries coming, so it should be fairly simple."

Lifting one shoulder in what Paul supposed was acceptance, Benson said, "It's the least I can do when you let me be underfoot like this, even when I'm not paying you for a room."

It was possibly the most earnest thing Benson had said to him, in addition to an expression of thanks after Paul had helped him resole his best pair of boots. He put down his pencil. He'd never wanted to pry, so he didn't know about Benson's circumstances outside of what he'd volunteered.

But he did consider him a friend and liked that he felt so at home here. Mother had never derided him, but she hadn't been as permissive with him, either. It wasn't best practice, for if someone else noticed the liberties Benson took, they might want them too.

Overall, Paul saw Benson as a large and good natured, if mystifying house cat. He preferred having him around, and not only because he was preternaturally inclined himself. Though Benson was perplexing and rarely smelled clean, he was calming, and he listened, and added something positive to his surroundings.

Paul could only imagine what was within his past, given how he looked, what he alluded to, and his reliance on middling but constant amounts of alcohol. There was talk of witches and witch-hunters, the latter his family had been. Whenever he made reference to ghosts, he did not seem to like them at all, and that was part of the rationale behind him staying in The Queen Anne at this moment.

"You look far off, lad," said Benson.

Paul ran a hand through his hair. "Sorry, did you say something else?"

"Before that?" Amused, Benson shook his head and fixed him with a fond, but tired glance. "Why are you fretting so?"

"You don't know I was fretting."

"What has you looking like you're miles from here, then?"

"I can't tell you." Though he suspected Lucas and Torquil were both still asleep, he couldn't promise they were. All would be compromised if Lucas in particular heard there wasn't anything to be found where he'd been told there was.

The largest problem at present concerned Lucas' source. He'd been tighter than wax about who it was, which didn't seem especially unusual for a man who made his living through illegal matters. Talking out of turn seemed ill-advised. Still, it nagged at Paul, and because it nagged at him, he wondered if it also nagged at Alastair.

Among other things, Paul longed to know if the source had known there was no treasure. Something like this could be some kind of set up, or so he thought.

But then, he had no idea what the point of that would be. He'd read so many novels, many of them called coarse by his mother, that the topics of smugglers and highwaymen were well fertilized within his imagination. He had little to compare the realities of crime to, aside from dramatic tales.

But he suspected they were usually more mundane, if anything Alastair barely said about it was an indication. Besides, truth was more grisly than fiction. It was impossible for Paul to visit Norwich without thinking about poor Martha Sheward, for example, whose husband had murdered her and left parts of her body around the city. The husband had lied, at first, telling police he thought she'd run away with some lover. When things like that were happening out in the world, it was difficult to say fiction was too sensationalist.

"Guard what you know, then," said Benson. He was, unless Paul missed his mark, completely unbothered.

"I would tell you if I trusted everyone under this roof. I'm not letting this happen again, I can tell you that much," Paul said.

"She'll look after you as well as you look after her," said Benson.

"Who?"

"Your pub. And I *am* helping with that, though protective magic is more delicate than we'd like it to be." Benson nodded to the mantelpiece. "I do keep charging them." Paul followed his eyes and considered the sigils on the wood, having little idea what any of them meant, but trusting Benson to have his best interests at heart.

Some might question that, he knew. Benson didn't appear very upstanding and Paul had seen young children cross the street to avoid him. "I appreciate it, all the same." He reflected upon how subtle it must have been. Benson being present did render a certain change in the air that had nothing to do with his scent, or the scent of his ominous drinks. Paul felt it as well as saw it, though he could only see it like dust motes flickering in the air. There one moment, gone if the light changed.

"How... can I ask, what does it do to deter ill intent?" He certainly didn't want Benson to be insulted, but he was curious. He thought again of his own penchant for listening to customers and how nothing had happened to punish him for it, concluding this must be because he didn't have any malicious reasoning when he did so.

"Haven't those newcomers been sleeping a lot?" Benson took up his dubious teacup again. "Haven't they been going out of The Queen Anne often?" He sipped, taking care to be daintier. "Don't they seem a little more affable than people forcing you to partake in crime should be?" He sipped again, still dainty. "Isn't it funny how you aren't dashing away *right* this moment?"

"Well... yes." He didn't know if it could be so simple. Simplicity could be deceiving, though. What he saw as simple was often dauntingly complex to others, whether that was his premonitions or the running of a public house.

"Potent magic is coercive, not flashy." Then Benson leaned closer to him and spoke just above a murmur. "And does your man have something a bit extreme in mind?"

Paul nodded mutely, meeting his eyes without any shame or remorse.

"But that's not what you can't tell me." He drew back.

"No," said Paul, sighing.

"I can't wait for you both to get back and regale me."

With a smile despite his headache, Paul realized Benson was sincere. He might not be able to see anything about the future, but his instincts were keen, and so it meant something to Paul if he said they would get back.

So it was that he felt a little less wary about their impending departure. As it would happen, and despite the rather alarming amount of strange things that had taken place of late, the rest of the day passed without incident. He hoped, as he fell asleep that night alongside Alastair's steady breathing, fortune would remain on their side.

THE LATE AFTERNOON LIGHT, dying as it pored over them, brought some calm to Alastair's spirit. If he'd known how full yet stilted the silence on the walk to Overstrand would be— they would pass through on their way to Trunch—he would've suggested Paul take a different route altogether. But Lucas wouldn't have allowed it and neither would Paul, in his loyal way. The prime difference was one of them had a gun and the other didn't.

"An old friend told me," said Lucas, and he sounded downright cheerful as they strode along, "that the East of England had all manner of smuggling, once upon a time. He said it was the only interesting thing about it."

The only things Alastair had known about this part of the world before he took residence here were general. Bert, likely the friend Lucas referenced, occasionally talked about the region and had kept a country house in Norfolk. Rather, his family had. It was apparently quite beautiful and featured local flint, although Bert was adamant that anybody with taste considered it too bucolic and small.

He'd mentioned using it between terms at, of course, Cambridge. Not being the sort of person who was invited to country houses, Alastair had never made the visit. Besides, their arrangement never merited clandestine country house liaisons. He scowled to himself. It *was* a bit amusing to consider how he now treaded paths Bert had mentioned with some derision.

His gilded life wasn't the one he'd wanted, evidently, and he'd longed to experience darker things. This was, apparently, why he'd moved north, stayed in the east and gone past York—which, if one believed him, was daring for a man of his set—into Edinburgh.

To Alastair, all of this seemed like an extension of privilege.

"So much," said Paul from behind him, and he was gladly called back to the task at hand by his voice. "I wouldn't have wanted to be a revenue man out here. Nobody would hear you scream. Or care, if they did." He paused; Alastair wanted to look back to see his face. "I hope you realize, Lucas, that it's going to take a bit more wandering and some tenacity to manage this."

Torquil, who was at Paul's side, cut in, oblivious to any tension. "That's why we have your man."

"I'm sure it's not the only reason why," said Paul, sounding admirably level. "You could manage to break and enter an abandoned house yourselves."

In response, Lucas did whip his head around and glare at Paul, his goodwill seemingly easy to puncture with droll humor. "Say that any louder and I'll make sure you quiet down, myself." The aggression wasn't very sensible; they had not passed anyone for some time and their surroundings were quiet and breeze-blown.

Alastair glanced at Paul, who was unrepentant. He hoped the smile in his eyes was enough to show he appreciated the remark. Then he elbowed Lucas roughly, though not enough to really stop him from walking. "You said it should be off on its own?"

"Yes," said Lucas, appearing to calm himself.

The four of them made their way along, and though Paul was more local and Alastair would have rather trusted him anyway, Lucas kept them to the main road. When they'd spoken about it back at The Queen Anne, upstairs and away from Paul—partially because Alastair demanded they keep the taproom itself as normal as possible, and also because Lucas was used to sharing his information and plans in secretive ways—Lucas gave the old farmhouse's location.

As cautiously as he could manage, Alastair had asked again who'd told Lucas about any of this, as well as why they volunteered the information.

Lucas did not want to say, even beyond a usual reticence to divulge anything of import. It felt far less necessary than any kind of secrecy Alastair had experienced while undertaking a job. By comparison, even awful, old Sykes had been more forthright than this, but Sykes had been moderately drunk during their interactions.

Knowing who'd enabled Lucas might matter more if what they sought existed. But because Alastair did not wish to think about Paul drowning, he almost wanted to believe the gold, the payment for long-forgotten ill gains, did exist. If he believed it did not, that belief strengthened the possibility of Paul's other vision being just as true as what he had seen and described underground. A cellar devoid of, well, anything.

At best, Paul might not die at the end of it. After all, he had not seen or felt death, precisely. Yet if James and Arthur were real, and the empty cellar was real, being thrown into chilling, dark water could be too. It all felt like a silent howl. Alastair had contemplated merely leading Lucas far enough down a disused road, then strangling him. The prospect was more alluring the less that Alastair felt in control of his circumstances.

Unfortunately, leading Lucas astray would be next to impossible.

Conversely, Torquil would have been a far easier and more suggestible target, but Alastair just planned on bribing him to silence and expected that would work. Though he was biddable and inexplicably cheerful, there seemed to be a nebulous disrespect lingering between him and Lucas. The latter seemed to keep Torquil's company largely because he was acquiescent and physically strong.

Torquil and Paul both bore canvas bags for their prize,

nondescript things that wouldn't attract any attention because they were used by workmen across various trades.

It didn't feel likely that Torquil would protest overmuch should Lucas be no longer with them, and he didn't seem the type to involve police. Alastair looked at him, thinking a more hardened man would consider killing him too. He didn't know if he'd always been softer than he imagined, but the longer he was near Paul, the less he was drawn to the more brutal paths his life had once presented.

13

The early evening journey to Trunch would have been rather beautiful, had it just been him and Alastair. Experienced walkers could probably have made it on foot from Overstrand in about two hours, and perhaps it was something they should keep in mind if they ever wanted to take a bit of time to themselves. When the weather was relatively mild, as it was even in late October, he'd gladly take such a ramble.

However, he, Lucas, Alastair, and Torquil had walked the bulk of the way, then paid a weathered old man with a cart to take them to the old road that led to the disused farm rumored to be favored for both illicit storage and meetings. If Lucas' information was correct, it had been. If Paul's vision was correct, it might've been, but it didn't matter.

The man, quite salt of the earth with deep wrinkles and a large, broad-brimmed hat, merely shrugged and nodded upon hearing their request. For all they knew, he might have been a local who'd known of such things a decade or two ago. Those operations had settled by then, the presence of most smugglers ebbing away as the laws had tightened, and relations with other countries shifted and changed legal trade agreements. But it would be naive to assume an older person possessed no ties to people who once had.

He told Paul he was passing that way anyway, so they may as well get in. Lucas and Torquil seemed rather confused by his accent, which would have been amusing to Paul had he been in a more lighthearted mood. He'd played translator, not for Alastair, but for them.

Paul had come this way before with his family, obviously not to any of the old smugglers' points they were trying to access now, but around the area and the village. Overstrand itself had rather infamous places that served as lookouts and landings because it was so close to the sea, as did Cromer. Trunch offered locations where goods were stored and sorted until they could be passed on to go elsewhere. It was slightly further inland, so the use made sense.

One particular story Paul had heard as a child—he'd never bothered looking for clippings to confirm the details because Grandfather assured him it was true—involved a foolhardy officer from the Custom House in Cromer who'd come to intercept some smugglers himself after hearing details of where they'd left their contraband. He thought they'd be an easy target, but that was hubris.

Instead of him stopping them from harvesting their illegally gotten gains, they tied him up and left him in a field by way of warning. According to what Paul had been told, the man was merely roughed up and jostled, not killed. But if he had been, it might have been omitted from the retelling, either by Grandfather or just because stories could lose their sharpness.

As it was now, Paul thought the old property they were presently approaching was rural enough for a body to go undiscovered for some time. He could see such a tale ending poorly for any revenue man going up against men who had every reason not to be caught.

The gloaming afforded them adequate light to see, but soon, they might need the candles secreted away in canvas bags meant to carry the valuables Lucas anticipated finding. Paul, to his quiet resentment, had one, Torquil the other.

He eyed the small farmhouse, noting that it did appear completely empty. Some of the windows were broken, both on the ground floor and the upper story. "Well, the house *is* here, at least," he remarked, not bothering to keep the irritation from his voice. "Not much to look at, is it?"

"We're not interested in the house," said Lucas, and it was a quick retort, but some eagerness had crept into his voice.

"There are at least a dozen ways you could have made money before coming all the way here for some dead smuggler's stuff," said Paul. He knew it, Alastair knew it, and Lucas must know it, too. It was exceedingly clear that this was more about punishing Alastair for the Adair matter. Nothing about it was particularly sensible or economical. At the least, it was a poor use of energy when one accounted for all the travel.

The only one who didn't grasp the pettiness of the matter might be Torquil, who offered, "Looks like there's an entrance to the cellar on the left side."

Paul surveyed the direction he indicated. The house wasn't remarkable in any way, and it was bordered by a lawn that had seen far better days, being full of tall and rather dry grass strewn with faint outlines of yellowed brown. It all stood on a slight hill, and before the trees on the hill had grown taller, the subtle rise might have been useful for lookout purposes.

The track they had used to get to the front of the house couldn't have been the only way to access it, not if it was used for clandestine drops, but overgrowth had obscured any other footpaths. Torquil was right, though. An unassuming brick outcropping on house's left bore small double doors, angled to accommodate what were likely stairs. Wordlessly, instinctively, Paul exchanged a look with Alastair, who had been uncharacteristically quiet as they'd loped to the house. Alastair gave him a fleeting and small smile, but Paul surmised he was busy cataloguing details—the state of the lawn, the hill's rise, how quiet it was. There were probably at least six things Alastair noticed that he didn't.

He sighed briefly through his nose. If he were to venture to Trunch, it wouldn't have been like this, and he certainly wouldn't be wandering down a worn dirt track that was this overgrown and faint just to get to an empty house, under which was supposedly a small network of little tunnels and cellars once used by local smugglers.

"Should we make sure no one is within?" Paul nodded at the house as he came to a halt beside Torquil.

With a scoff, Lucas said, "Does it look like anyone is inside?"

"It's a wonder you haven't been arrested before now," said Paul. "What if there is? Isn't it better not to take the chance?"

Lucas shook his head. "Rich talk coming from the likes of you. You two always look like lovers on a stroll. Wonder *you've* never been arrested."

He shouldn't have said it; Alastair was larger than him, and he'd been admirably compliant while Lucas had been around and interfering in his life, but he didn't appear keen on letting such a remark pass without rebuke. Paul watched mutely as Alastair leaned closer to Lucas, using his stature to loom over him, and murmured, "I'd watch your tongue." He landed a punch—a love tap for them, Paul imagined—to the side of Lucas' face.

Lucas, stubborn to the last, responded with a quick jab up that connected with Alastair's lower lip. It was fascinating to watch two men who'd likely scrapped their way through life do so with such... efficiency? Paul wanted to know if he could ever learn to move so gracefully; though boxing was not at all genteel, they made it look nearly like ballet and this wasn't even a real fight.

Then Lucas stepped back, quickly, and withdrew the gun he carried somewhere under his overcoat. Paul hadn't gotten near enough to him to figure out exactly where he'd stashed it, but he knew it was there both from the vision and pragmatic assumptions. "I'll say what I want, I think."

He leveled the gun at Paul, who thought about feigning a yawn but didn't wish to goad him. He didn't think he was going to die this way, and he didn't quite think he was going to be injured, either. It was still better not to take the chance. He'd never had a man point a weapon at him, so he took his cues from Alastair. Besides, the sensation of being under such a threat was quite strange and unnerving, even if it did seem just for show. It felt meant to prove he could draw Paul into this precise situation and possibly pull the trigger.

Alastair shook his head, but did back down. "We're almost finished. Then you can be on your way."

"Might stop over in your lovely establishment on my way back home," said Lucas, as though Torquil wasn't there at all.

"I'll be happy to have such a newly wealthy customer," said Paul, his eyes back on Lucas' and not the barrel of the small gun. The dying light still gave them enough to see as the gloaming retreated into proper night, and the barrel's metal looked impossibly dark to Paul.

Meanwhile, the location and the circumstances put him in the mood to think about creatures like Old Shuck; he could understand why, whether it was part of the waking, real world or not, it was said to haunt the region. Even without the looming old house, the landscape itself felt eerie, permeated with energies that might drive a man to awful things.

Perhaps a great black dog would make an appearance and do away with them, including Lucas. Old Shuck had to hate it when anybody wandered around his land, and Paul imagined all of this was. He slid his glance to Alastair, whose face was as furious as he had ever seen it. He wondered if Alastair might even try to tackle Lucas right this moment. He could likely do it without incident.

But as Paul took in the fury that was evident in his eyes and the set of his jaw, paired with the way he resolutely did not move, he realized: just as Lucas had been purposefully antagonizing him, Alastair wanted Lucas to feel some hope just before he was cornered and dealt with. It would make his ultimate demise all the sweeter, or so Paul assumed.

He couldn't decide how he felt about that, but he had never been part of these circles. It might not be for him to have a decided opinion. He didn't have particular opinions on how to make shirts, either, because he didn't have the faintest notion how in the first place.

After a sly smile, Lucas seemed to decide he'd directly

threatened Paul enough and put away his weapon. He said, "I like your spirit."

Not giving him an inch, Paul said, "It seems to vex you, but there's no accounting for taste and some men like to be vexed."

"Rather than tease each other," said Alastair, "shall we get into the cellar and take what we came for?" He patted Lucas on the back roughly. "Doesn't seem anyone will be able to tell if we do light our wee candles, so let's get on with it."

As he withdrew short, cheap candles from the bag, Paul tried not to seem too coiled and nervous. He trusted Alastair, but the fact remained that Lucas was armed, and he was not, and they'd be going underground. The cellar might not be stable, any tunnels even less so. When he considered the irregular marks on the lawn, he wondered if they might indicate where the cellar ran. But he was wildly out of his depth, so he handed two of the candles to Alastair instead of contemplating that any further. Paul looked up and into his eyes when he touched his palm in the handoff.

"I've got matches in my pocket," he said, smiling in such a subtle way that only Paul could notice it.

Moderately placated, Paul took a breath when he lit his candle, then touched the wick to the second and passed it to Lucas more carelessly. That finished, Paul took another candle and held it out for Alastair to light. Torquil seemed content enough without one, but since they'd be standing watch outside together, it didn't matter if he had his own. Naturally, he was also supposed to be minding Paul, who couldn't alert any authorities with expediency even if he tried.

That had always been the location's whole point, after all.

The supposed revenue man's hubris was evidence of it; Paul supposed it might be simple for more than one smuggler to overtake one man set out to stop all of them. But in addition, there was no straightforward way to summon any help. Not unless one could make it up the track, to the road, and all the way back to the village. The nearest neighbor couldn't be seen from here, even if the trees were short enough to grant a better line of sight from here on the rise. At one point in time, they must have been.

"Right," said Lucas, "you two wait here. I don't expect this will take long."

From your lips to God's ears, thought Paul, although he didn't actually have much use for God. Silently, he passed his bag to Alastair and Torquil did the same to Lucas. He resisted the urge to kiss Alastair—there'd be time enough for that, later.

THE CELLAR DOORS came open with a puff of dust and released a sweet whiff of water-damaged wood. They weren't, however, doors to the cellar. Lucas snarled, frustrated, but Alastair just chuckled.

"It would've been too easy," he said, as they both looked at some kind of large and empty cupboard. From some feet away behind them, he heard Paul shuffle on the worn track. He knew the rustle of his clothes and shoes. "Honestly, that does bode well. If it's so important, they wouldn't have risked an obvious entrance, would they?"

"Suppose not," said Lucas. He stepped back from Alastair

and glanced at the house. "Bet there's a cellar door near the stairs. Come on."

Heedless of the house's disrepair, he tried a side door to the left of what they faced, wrenching at the knob. Though the door was old, it didn't give. With apparent relish, he gave it a well-placed kick, the upper half of his body remaining still and straight enough that the candle didn't flicker much beyond what it would in a normal draft and the large canvas bag merely shuddered a little. Lucas was still in fit enough shape, Alastair reckoned. His posture indicated so.

It wouldn't matter; he wasn't going to fight him. He wouldn't give him the chance. Though many might believe in honorable killing, in not doing things while someone's back was turned, Alastair believed more in staying alive and defending himself than honor.

The door swung forward with a quiet squeak of hinges, revealing a dark room or corridor within. At a guess, it probably led to the kitchen or a mudroom. Without waiting to be told, because he knew he would be going first whether or not he wanted to, Alastair preceded him.

Lucas wouldn't try to shoot him until they reached what he thought was the goal of their journey, namely forgotten, ill-gotten gains of one sort or another. He might not try to shoot Alastair at all, or he might attempt to kill him at the end of all this. The thought had crossed his mind, only in that idle way of contemplating what he knew of Lucas.

Taking a breath as his eyes adjusted to the darkness inside the house, he took them through a lonely, empty kitchen. A small, hot dribble of wax landed on the side of his hand and he appreciated the sensation. It kept him where he needed to be.

Thinking it could serve as a bludgeon if he needed it, he picked up a dense, nondescript brass candlestick from a dusty shelf as he passed and gently settled his candle in the base. Somebody had no doubt just left it, for it wasn't at all valuable. It was just the type of sturdy, dependable object a farmer or a smuggler—both pragmatic people, in their ways—would keep around.

"Think it's been empty for ages," remarked Alastair, taking into account the amount of dust and the heaviness of the air. Perhaps he was just a fanciful man, too, for the house felt to him like it had a bit of personality. Rather like The Queen Anne did. This one felt shy and retiring, like it didn't mind they were inside, but it didn't want to volunteer too much.

Lucas only grunted, seemingly intent upon his goals rather than making any chatter. It didn't stop Alastair from chattering, however.

"Here," said Alastair, as they came upon an entryway, "there's the front door." He crept across a wooden floor that creaked from disuse, even at his practiced steps. "The foot of the stairs is here..."

Examining them, he went to the base and spotted the outline of a door set into the wooden panels. He was no expert on history or architecture, but he'd guess the place had probably been built two or three hundred years before, then had renovations or additions over time. It didn't seem any larger on the inside than it had looked as they approached, and it wasn't a grand manor. Someone, though, had lived here quite comfortably once upon a time.

"There we go," said Alastair, and Lucas all but leapt forward to snatch at the doorknob. "Steady on—anything behind that door might not even be passable." Not that he particularly cared; if Lucas fell through some rotted stairs and snapped his neck, it would solve many of his present problems. He hadn't even pointed out the faint marks on the lawn that might mean cellars or rooms built underground.

He hadn't been sure Lucas had noticed them, as eager as he was. Here he stood, plainly assuming that he'd get what he wanted and all that stood between him and it was an old door. Alastair wanted to pause and now demand who'd put him up to this in the first place; it seemed like some of their information was correct and that was a small surprise to him. He'd almost expected there to be nothing on this track outside Trunch, which he'd only seen on maps.

Under sweeter circumstances, he could see rambling to the village with Paul. As things were, he couldn't wait to leave.

Rather than impede Lucas from opening the door, he stepped slightly out of the way. When it opened to reveal a set of steps trailing down into soft, deep darkness, Lucas said, "Go."

Sighing, Alastair held his candle aloft and descended. He wasn't convinced of the structural integrity of anything beyond this point, knowing well what sort of measures criminal operations took and that they were centered on stealth as much as survival. But he did proceed.

The first step groaned with his weight, but it held. So did the next, and the next. As he descended, none of them gave or snapped or showed signs of rot, for which he was thankful. He had no plans to die, or to let Lucas kill or injure him, but a broken ankle or limb due to shoddy wood was more out of his control. He couldn't help but breathe a sigh of relief when he reached the floor, which seemed far more trustworthy.

Lucas had followed him eagerly, perhaps less worried about something giving way under him.

Angling the candle so he could see, the room was unremarkable and not as low or close as he might have imagined. It was a good-sized cellar, and it still featured a few boxes and barrels. Preserved vegetables and fruits, their forms and identities long lost to time, lined some shelves set into the walls.

He knew if there was some kind of entrance to tunnels or other rooms used for more nefarious things than food, it would probably be hidden to anyone who didn't know how to look for it. Lucas was likely having similar thoughts to his. He raised his candle, heedless of the wax dripping onto his hand, and examined the walls.

"A door could also be behind something. Easier to hide, and the less intelligent revenue man might miss it if it were hidden with something that looked heavy," Alastair said, going to the shelves across the cellar, which weren't set into the wall like the others. He thought it was also possible that bribes could have been exchanged.

"True..."

Alastair tapped with the heels of his boots as he went, fairly satisfied the floor was just dirt and not wood disguised, or lost, under dirt. It did sound solid, not hollow in any manner. "If I was one of those bastards a hundred years ago, I would have built out from the cellar and not down. Down would leave more potential for collapsing, and if you die smothered, you can't spend anything."

"I wouldn't think there's more beneath us, no," murmured Lucas. Seemingly even Lucas could admit when someone else was right, and he had respected Alastair for all they'd not really gotten along. It had been the matter with Adair that rendered him more of an outright antagonist, it seemed. He came nearer to Alastair and cocked his head at the same set of shelves. "This is like that bar your lad has in his taproom. Smaller, though."

"It was an apothecary's counter before they moved it inside, he told me," said Alastair, wondering why he was volunteering the information and unable to stop himself, "but you're right."

It did look similar to the bar in The Queen Anne's taproom, but he suspected that just meant they were from the same era. There was no long counter, but the back had the same rows of shelves, one at a height where it would be comfortable for most men to rest their forearms.

Almost immediately in his examinations, he spotted a subtle, but innocent, groove in the outermost frame of the thing, almost like a decorative indent nearly at his eye level. There was a symmetrical one on the frame's other side, but it wasn't as smooth and it was right next to the corner of the cellar. Anything that slid to the side, or especially swung out toward a person, would need a little more room to function.

Lucas frowned at him. "Well, whatever it is, I haven't the faintest fucking idea how anybody got it down here."

To Alastair, it looked as though it could have been built specifically for the cellar, which meant it would have been made or finished in the space. But he didn't say so. He strode to it and put his free palm on the shelves' frame, running it down to the groove. Pressing it gently, he made as though to push it toward the corner, much like one might slide a door on a track.

At the precise moment when he thought he might be wrong, the shelf did finally give and slide over, though not without an unholy squeak. The opening in the wall wasn't very large—at one time, he reckoned the shelves could move more—but both he and Lucas would be able to pass through.

"I was hoping you'd be wrong," said Lucas, as Alastair stepped back and favored him with a smug glance. "You keep being right."

"Of course you didn't hope so," he said, "you brought me along for a reason, right?" Without waiting to be told, he stepped forward and into the new darkness.

14

————

Night was falling, and minutes felt like they were taking ten for every one. Paul tried to count himself lucky that Torquil was innocuous, or he would be if he hadn't accompanied a more worrisome criminal to undertake this particular errand.

"It really is supposed to be money down there," said Torquil, his voice slipping into the autumnal lull of scattered nightbirds' calls.

Paul took a chance, believing if either Lucas or Torquil were to speak on the matter, it would be Torquil. "Even if it is, why not make money some other way? I haven't much notion of what you'd consider your trade—"

"Thieving," Torquil supplied.

"Right." Paul glanced down at him. Torquil had sat on a large rock just opposite the house, one that afforded a good view of the lawn. "This is still a lot of trouble for something that's not promised, isn't it? When you could have planned something that was a little more sure?"

One day, he was sure he'd think about all of this more

seriously, but at present, his nerves were too taxed for too much thinking to be either possible or attractive. He wanted Alastair safe; he wanted them back in their room under the covers. The last issues he wished to consider were how the criminal world usually conducted its business, or why some of its members might choose to do one thing over another.

He was still adjusting to Alastair's multitudinous past; it didn't change the depth of his regard. But he'd realized in recent weeks that the depth of his regard was only matched by the depth of the life Alastair had lived. His own life, by comparison, felt woefully linear for all the preternatural was involved.

"It's more than the money," said Torquil.

He appeared to deliberate slightly before saying more, and Paul was content to wait. Torquil seemed relatively companionable, or like he would be if he was allowed to be. While Paul assumed Lucas might shoot at will, the same might not be said of his compatriot: not only had Paul not seen Torquil wield a gun, so he wasn't positive Torquil had one at all, his temperament also felt different.

It made Paul recognize how many types of people were drawn to, or perhaps slipped into, criminal activities for their survival or benefit. He'd never really believed all of them were categorically bad, the way some learned folks did seem to suggest, and he felt things like phrenology were ridiculous. Seeing Alastair, Torquil, and Lucas together made him question the criminal as a type even more. They might comport themselves similarly in a given situation, but that was learned.

One might be able to hazard a guess that Lucas' scar on his face wasn't a normal accident, but most people would not jump to something like a knife fight being the reason it was there. Alastair was dripping in tattoos, but sailors had them too. Torquil was a pleasant enough fellow, and his features were unremarkable. In addition, his manner of dress didn't mark him one way or the other.

"What else is it, then?"

Hesitating, Torquil looked up at him.

"You can tell me. Once this is all through, I don't plan on seeing either of you again, and I'm certain Alastair won't want to renew any friendships he had with you. If that's even the right word."

Paul put on his best jovial landlord face, the sort that most customers would speak to. Edward had always done it a little better because he was naturally gregarious; if he and Alastair ever met, they'd get on wonderfully. But Paul knew he was good at it, too. He was just a little more genteel and less effusively warm.

"Lucas' source," said Torquil, "is somebody your man knows."

"I'm sure he knows a lot of people."

"I don't think I was supposed to hear most of it," said Torquil, "but it was late and the pub was almost empty, and nobody told me to go away, so I was just sitting and drinking while they talked by the fire."

"Lucas and this source?"

"His name is Bert. He's some rich man, and he sounds more like you when he talks, sometimes. Except I heard him say he went to Cambridge, so he's got that real fancy way about him. Even the way he speaks, you know?"

Nodding, Paul clutched his candle. It wasn't burning too low, yet, but in retrospect, he didn't know why they'd bothered to have them up here. The sky wasn't dark as pitch and the sky was clear. There was still enough light to see, at least aboveground.

"Well, they're talking of old times, and they get on the topic of Alastair. They both knew him. And this Bert, he's had a little to drink, it's late, and he's slumming it, ain't he? So he gets sort of emotional, especially after Lucas tells him about the shit with Adair—the burglary not going to plan. That's how I learned about the stuff with Adair, by the way."

Paul didn't care much about that detail. "Lucas told this Bert he thought Alastair was to blame for there being nothing to steal?"

"Yes, he said he'd known about that Alice girl, and Alastair bringing her back to her father." Torquil gazed at the house, no doubt wondering if his talking about all of this would bring Lucas forth faster. Paul didn't have the heart to tell him that only one person should be coming back. The quandary of what to do with Torquil came back into his mind. He was sure Alastair had already thought about it, and he hoped bribery would be the answer. "He was just waiting for the right time to do something."

Lucas meant nothing to him, and neither did Torquil, but only one of them had shown himself to be wantonly invested in causing Alastair trouble. Paul watched Torquil watch the house. No, this one was being dragged along. "What did Bert say to that? It'd been years ago, hadn't it? Why did either of them care?"

"Lucas cared because he hated being crossed. But I don't think it sounds so bad. I've heard of friends betraying each other, going to the police with information... then someone ends up hanged or jailed." Torquil shrugged. "Alastair didn't do that. Seems like he didn't expect to be rewarded, or for the old man to ruin their break-in. If I were Lucas, I'd have let it go. Nobody got caught. Nobody died."

Paul found himself smiling faintly. "I wish Lucas saw it that way."

"So do I," said Torquil. "I'm not cut out for travel and here I am, dragged into his grudge. Anyway, Bert hears all of that, and he says, 'That sounds like Alastair; he's prone to fancies.' And…" Almost warily, Torquil paused. "I don't mean any offense, but Bert is like you."

"Like me?" Paul didn't understand. He had nothing in common with anybody who went to Cambridge, except, apparently, an accent that Bert did his best to shed or hide.

"Like you and Alastair. He prefers men."

That followed; Cambridge had that reputation. Perhaps he did have something in common with Cambridge boys. "I see."

Seemingly satisfied that Paul wasn't offended, Torquil went on. "He told Lucas they had been lovers, and he thought it'd meant something to Alastair. As much as it meant to him. Bert said they'd meet up whenever he came through Edinburgh. But one day, when he set out to do that, Bert found he had gone. There was no note, nothing—only some cross, quiet charlady who answered Alastair's door."

That must have been after Alastair left James. It begged the question of whether Bert had met James, but Paul didn't assume so. No, chances were, the woman had merely answered the door for a caller and turned him away.

It would be easy after that for Bert to conclude Alastair was no longer in residence if there were no replies to any notes, or perhaps said charlady had mentioned it herself.

Eyeing the dark clusters of trees some feet away from where they stood near the empty house, Paul sighed.

The idea that Alastair had taken other lovers was not unexpected, but he found himself resentful toward someone he'd never even met. "Had Lucas figured out Alastair was in Cromer, by the time you overheard all this?"

Brightly, almost, Torquil said, "Yes. We'd talked to the boy —the son—and that baker." Paul could imagine James was eager to offer details to any men who appeared ready to inconvenience his father. "Lucas *told* Bert this was where Alastair had gone. I don't know if Lucas *wanted* Bert to swoop down and cause trouble, but he did say Alastair was in Cromer. He gave Bert the name of your place, too. We expected him to be there by the time we showed up."

In turn, they had received that information from James. "Haven't had any customers called Bert or Albert that I know of," said Paul, turning all of these new details over in his mind. "Nobody that's stayed the night, anyway. He might've been in the taproom." Not everyone who wanted a drink gave their names, after all.

"Bert asked Lucas if he wanted a way to make Alastair's life a little bit worse for a while, and Lucas said yes. Lucas and Alastair... they were friends, but I guess the sort of friends who might fight. Alastair was before my time, though." Torquil frowned. "If you don't mind me saying so, he's not the best to work with."

None of Lucas and Torquil's shared background was of interest to Paul.

With a controlled tone of curiosity that did not belie how much he wanted to know more about Bert, he said, "I understand. Bert gave Lucas the story of lost loot and this location."

The man must be something of a local; perhaps he'd been born nearby in some country house or manor, or perhaps he'd made a study of the folklore and the stories. Stranger things had happened. "Because it's here and close to The Queen Anne. Well, relatively."

Torquil's reply was not unexpected. "Aye. All of it," he said. "Bert said something about some relative getting caught near here. I'm not best with details, but he was the one who told Lucas all about it. Assured him he knew the area, knew the history, and if Lucas was so inclined, he might be able to drag Alastair into something sort of messy—and make a bit of coin."

Abruptly, Paul thought he understood with clarity why and how there was no loot. The secret cellars existed, and the farmhouse had very likely been used as a place to stow things transported away from landing and drop points. Maybe Bert did have a free-trading relation who had gotten in trouble here. It wouldn't really matter, as the stories themselves abounded, mingling with legal record and known facts.

Bert could direct anybody to the house because it was there, knowing full well that there was no money.

Paul had to admit it was an elegant, if a complex and stealthy, way to make someone's life more complicated for at least a little while.

There was even the possibility of Alastair being physically hurt or killed, particularly since Lucas had held such a grudge.

This Bert, whoever he was, probably thought little of Lucas—or, if he thought well of him, he didn't mind causing him some grief. He wanted Alastair to suffer, somehow, and being sent on a fool's errand wasn't torture or maiming or murder, but it was certainly inconvenient and risky in its way. It would also unearth past decisions, things Alastair had kept buried.

Honestly, thought Paul, it was a devious suggestion to have made. One couldn't know for certain that anything would be taken to its fullest extent, because Lucas might decide not to go to England at all, or Alastair might choose not to engage with him even if he did.

Bert might have a hunch more is at stake.

Paul was landlord of The Queen Anne, which was on public records, and Alastair might have mentioned him by name in a letter. There would be no mention of their relationship, such as it was, but if one were that way inclined, as Bert was—*and* he believed he'd been spurned—it would be easy to conjecture that perhaps Paul signified something to Alastair other than just an employer.

Certainly, someone who let slip stories about Norfolk smugglers in the hopes they'd embroil a past lover in such an oblique way might be paltry or delusional enough to assume much. There was no accounting for the upper echelons and their capacity for dramatics, or so he'd come to conclude after years of overhearing those employed by them.

Alastair might prefer being beaten in an alley to all of this, if payback was truly the end intention. Better the straightforward message than the twisted one.

At last, feeling Torquil's eyes on him as he remained quiet, he said, "Sounds like this Bert is a little conniving."

"Conniving?"

"Oh. Up to something."

That, Torquil apparently understood far better. He nodded. "Lucas said they'd known each other since they were lads, so I didn't say anything. But it felt to me like he wanted something out of Lucas." Slowly, he added, "He blathered *a lot* about Alastair, I can say. But how could they be in love? Different sorts of people, for one, and I mean from separate worlds."

More separate than Alastair's and his own, that was for sure. Paul held his tongue as Lucas went on. "How would a man like Alastair sit at one of those fancy meals with all the forks and get on well? He couldn't even attend as a friend and make it convincing, could he? All the rules in society... you've got to grow up learning those, haven't you?"

A reluctant chuckle left Paul. He thought Alastair was heartbreakingly elegant, but he knew what Torquil meant. He said, "And apart from that, it would be a bit difficult to carry on some grand love affair if one party is expected to take a wife, which I should think Bert is supposed to have. Money, property, all that has to go to someone."

Many rich men who took other men as lovers, especially ones of a different station, probably didn't think it mattered if they married. They could conduct themselves in private as they chose.

He didn't want to think of Alastair being trapped in such an arrangement, particularly when he'd already had something of a sham marriage. It was so clear that he wanted to be loved equitably, and fully, and being part of something in secret would not appeal to him in any way.

"I'm glad you said it and not me," said Torquil.

Paul inclined his head and offered a slight smile. "You're not offending me by stating facts. Anyway, your boss has offended me far more by careening into my life and pointing a gun at me. We haven't even *really* discussed such things."

There had been that odd little exchange in the kitchen, but it hadn't been centered on either taunts or platitudes about preferring men. Lucas didn't seem to have a particular objection to anyone's desires, including his own. He just seemed opportunistic and bitter.

"That does seem worse, on balance, than who wants to bed who. The gun."

Yes, when Alastair emerged—and he would—Paul would convince him that Torquil didn't need to be dealt with quite so harshly as Lucas, if that was indeed what Alastair was thinking. He wasn't a loose end so much as a malleable loose cannon.

THE AIR SMELLED SICKLY, and cobwebs more like gauze had gathered in the edges of the corridor behind the sliding shelves. The ceiling was somewhat lower than the cellar's, but that was to be expected from something that had been hurriedly or crudely dug out. Alastair ducked his head slightly as he walked. Lucas, who was shorter, would have less trouble and could probably stand straight.

People had not been here for quite some time. He sneezed, no doubt at the smell, dust in the air, and the presence of mold. A cold drip of water fell on his nose, having missed his hat. He said, as he continued to walk within the light of his gently guttering candle, "Let's get this done with."

The lack of watertightness as well as the soft draft had him thinking this wasn't a particularly sound place to be walking in, if it ever had been, and he didn't appreciate the thought of being smothered in a collapse. His mother had told him a story out of Richmond, that of a little drummer boy who'd been sent by some soldiers to investigate a tunnel between Easby Abbey and the castle.

The boy drummed along and the soldiers followed him aboveground, until suddenly, the drumming stopped in the woods. Rather than find a way to investigate what had happened, much less rescue him, they abandoned him entirely, too afraid of what might have claimed him below to try anything.

As a man, Alastair saw how it was far more likely the boy had tripped and hit his head, walked into some bit of rock that stuck out from the top of the tunnel and stunned himself, or possibly fallen into some unseen, deep drop.

As a boy, he was certain the little drummer boy had been attacked by a hellhound or some trolls. The cowardice of the soldiers made sense, because he understood how they wouldn't want to run into such a terrible, preternatural creature. The least, he'd thought, the soldiers could do was look for the boy.

He had long since stopped trusting men with power or weapons to do the right thing, and being in a tunnel now, he found he was more likely to believe in the hellhound than a death by natural causes. This might have been because he presently cohabitated with a seer and had a friend who saw the ghost of his dead wife, all in a region of England said to be haunted by Old Shuck.

He didn't enjoy the sensation of being here at all. He had been in parts of the vaults in Edinburgh—in cellars that once connected to them, anyway. They hadn't been as oppressive as this narrow stretch of rather putrid smelling darkness.

Then again, you never had to live in the vaults. He brushed aside all thoughts of the poor souls who had resorted to living under the South Bridge, knowing he was only letting his imagination run freely.

He squinted and saw a looming, darker patch just ahead. He assumed it led to another room, for it looked wider than the corridor itself. The ground was reassuringly dense, so he didn't fear he'd fall through anything. A handful of measured steps brought him to the mouth of a second cellar, this one appearing more primitive than the first.

Just as Paul had said, it was empty. So he stepped inside, ducking his head slightly, and waited for Lucas to draw nearer and see it for himself.

"Mate, there's nothing here," said Alastair, after a pause. He flinched away from a cobweb that brushed his mouth. "Sorry, but I think your man had bad information. Or he just got something wrong. That *can* happen—these old stories, you know."

"Or you just got here first." Lucas must have realized it was nonsense to claim so. They had all been under The Queen Anne's roof over the last few days, and Paul and Alastair had been together for long stretches only at night. It might be possible for one to go to Trunch and back in that time, but visibility would be terrible and there was no telling how they'd have arranged it.

Alastair let Lucas be angry. The noises he made in the back of his throat sounded like some scuffling woodland creature that was about to strike.

"How the fuck would I have done that?"

"You and that boy of yours," said Lucas. "You two could've managed something. He's uncanny, that one, and he's local.

Has all sorts of knowledge, I'd bet, and this damn village has more than one cellar, more than one—"

Not patient enough to allow Paul to be called *boy*, Alastair said, "Careful what you say next."

"You did it before." Then, Lucas looked around as though he might notice a chest or some boxes that were not and would not be there. He paced a bit, clearly agitated.

"I just did a good deed, and someone repaid me for it," Alastair said dismissively. "I didn't go out of my way to cheat you. Not then, not now."

"But that Apollyon. I trust him even less than I trust you."

It was true that Paul struck most people as different. It wasn't entirely tangible, and he doubted anyone would be able to explain why he struck them like a Druid or a prophet, but it was present in his demeanor. He was, of course. Sort of. Not a Druid, if they were real, but something of a prophet.

Alastair, who was used to these reactions by now, said, "Why'd you even come all this way to exact your revenge, then? You seemed to trust me to help you with whatever the fuck this was supposed to be."

With the most peeved of scowls, Lucas fell quiet, and Alastair looked around, taken despite himself with the thought of smugglers building such a space. The walls all looked solid enough, but one of them might obscure another passageway. If, naturally, things hadn't collapsed or become obstructed.

"You're not a child," Alastair said. "You should have known better. You just wanted to make my life difficult, and you knew I was in Cromer, so when you heard anything to do with Norfolk... you jumped at the thought of dragging me into it."

"I would've come myself. With Torquil. You being near, that was an added incentive to do it."

His weakening tone tugged at Alastair's curiosity, at his suspicions that this wasn't really done just for potential material gain. The possibility would be attractive to someone like Lucas, always, but Alastair's sense that there was more to it was stronger than ever in this forgotten room under the earth.

Alastair offered, "This type of shit... it's all just stories. Somebody tells somebody who tells somebody. *If* there was anything here, it's been gone. For what it's worth, I didn't really think there'd be anything at all." Lucas drew his gun. Without any malice, Alastair murmured something he knew wasn't true, for *he* had wanted to take advantage of the location's obscurity, after all. "You won't. You'd get found out."

Men like them were usually afraid of consequences, though one would be hard-pressed to get them to admit it.

"You'd rot down here." Nary a tremble in his voice, though it seemed tight with annoyance, Lucas stepped closer to him.

Left unspoken was the second implication of the words: for Alastair to rot, Paul would have to be killed, too. If he were left alive, authorities would be sent to retrieve the body and possibly capture Lucas.

It chilled Alastair more than the possibility of his own demise.

He glanced down at the little gun levelled at his torso. "Mind the floor. It's not even."

"Just shut the fuck up," said Lucas. The words weren't loud, but they were charged. "You lucky bastard who can't seem to do anything wrong—gone from the gutter to being safe and warm. And wanted. You're no different from me." Quiet, for Alastair had thought such things himself in the dead of night when nobody was able to stop him from ruminating, he waited for Lucas to finish growling. "But, somehow, you get whatever you want."

If envy propelled Lucas, Alastair couldn't quite blame him. It was a little late to talk things through, but he felt he owed it to a dead man walking to let him express his frustration. And he still wanted to know one thing. "Who told you to come here? The person with the grandfather or the great-grandfather or the cousins... whoever?"

During the little tête-à-têtes they'd had in his room at The Queen Anne, Lucas hadn't supplied a name. Often, their work didn't require one, and indeed it could be dangerous to trade in names. But now, Alastair was more than inquisitive.

Caught off-guard, perhaps believing Alastair didn't really care enough to ask directly because he had given up trying, Lucas said, "Doesn't matter."

"Christ, man," said Alastair. "It does. I didn't set you up—I mean, I didn't sneak here in the dead of night with my lover and empty the place. Didn't even know it existed until you said."

Ruefully, he thought the work he'd done for Sykes hadn't ever extended to this level of effort. Mostly, he had just sat in pubs like The Bell and secured people who wanted to buy lifted goods. Sykes hadn't been good at much, but somehow he'd managed to arrange the storage and sale of things that weren't his or their buyers'—stolen jewelry, gold, expensive liquor, fancy curios.

The cut Alastair had received had been welcome, though not particularly necessary. Mostly, he'd been bored in his wanderings and wanted something to occupy his time. He hadn't realized until he'd arrived how extensive free trading had been in Norfolk, or how it had shifted into quieter and smaller affairs that were far more mundane.

Really, he should have known, given the coast bordered the North Sea and the Broads could be used in the same manner as roads.

He added, "I don't need much money beyond what I've got, as you well know. Neither does Paul, really. We're not greedy." He took a short breath. "Who told you? Could they have lied?" Neither of them would have any illusions of everybody being truthful, and Alastair just wanted Lucas to consider it.

The gun drooped, its barrel now pointing at the floor. Alastair would rather it didn't point near his foot, but he could deal with an injured foot more successfully than a hole in his stomach.

Lucas said, "You... shit, you think he *knew* there was nothing here? All this was on purpose?"

Alastair understood *he* meant the source, not Paul, at this point in the discussion. Lucas sounded rather stunned at the thought, and Alastair wanted to say he should have considered the possibility. But everyone made mistakes, some worse than others, and if Lucas was motivated by pettiness as much as a desire for money, well, such an emotion would fetter most logic.

Tilting his head in the barest nod, Alastair said, "It's possible. Some men like to have fun at others' expense. Others just like to lie. Tell me who it was. Do I know him?" He hadn't known many people from this part of England, or with knowledge of it, but there were a few.

Taking several deep breaths before he spoke, making his own candle's flame tremble, Lucas muttered, "It was Bert."

There was only one Bert he knew personally, and Lucas knew him too; it had to be the same one. Especially uttered in that resigned tone. Especially if Alastair had thought about him too, if only earlier today. Alastair peered at him, but could not summon much astonishment. "Bert Calder?"

"He's mad for you," said Lucas. "Thinks you're the love of his life."

"I usually had the impression he was just excited to sleep with someone like me." It was not fully true, not if he reached and examined all he had felt and thought around Bert. Nonetheless, Bert had seemed quite intrigued by their differences in social status.

"One night, he came round The Sow and we talked over pints." The Sow had been their favored, dirty, regular public house. "Like old times, you know, only he's got all his family's money now. His brother died of some fucking fever, so he finally *actually* inherited. But as it happened, we didn't end at just talking." With a mirthless smirk, Lucas shrugged. "And here I am."

Maybe Alastair wouldn't kill him, after all. He wouldn't ever trust him or leave him alone in a room with Paul, but he mightn't need to turn to murder. He held a little pity, even after everything.

After trying to reconcile this new information and failing, he said, "Can we talk about this topside? I can't tell if it's the dust, or the fact you've just told me he's *mad* for me, that has me feeling queasy." He briefly thought it might be fun to see how Paul reacted to hearing some man from his past was apparently mad for him. Then he addressed the matter of

Lucas' gun. "Are you gonna shoot me so that I bleed out? I'd prefer you didn't."

Giving a half-hearted snarl, Lucas put it away. "I might've. But now that you've mentioned he might've known how nothing was here, I'd rather just break his nose and all his toes for goading me into coming all this way. I've known him since we were lads, but you got to know him better than me— you're probably correct. He's such a smug little fucker, ain't he?"

A kind thing to say might have been something along the lines of, it was easy to mislead anyone with the right information. But Alastair still believed that Lucas' grudge against him had left Lucas easy to manipulate.

Now that it had been confirmed, Alastair could imagine how Bert maneuvered him into doing all of this. They had been boyhood friends, after all. Or as much as someone who'd been brought up by a mad butcher, and someone else whose parents had everything, could be. But it was evident that they'd bonded.

Perhaps Lucas, who'd been both hotheaded and shrewd as long as Alastair knew him, found something attractive about Bert's relative guilelessness. He was spoiled, but he hadn't been worldly or jaded. *I'll have to ask how they met.* He had taken it for granted, and it was obvious that Lucas wasn't sleeping with him.

Bert was annoying, just a bit simpering and over-eager, but he'd been tolerated and kept out of trouble by their scraggy little group. It helped that he always volunteered to pay for their drinks, and occasionally, he was known to pay for certain other vices.

"That's all right," said Alastair, "I was planning to kill you once we got down here, anyway. Probably by bashing your head against something, or... I don't know, using the candlestick as a bludgeon. You were right. I don't think anyone would find a body until it was in a disgusting state. If they did at all."

Though he was certain they'd never be friends, not of the sort he wished to have, it was a great relief when Lucas burst into laughter.

15

———

Two notable things happened on the way home from Trunch: he and Alastair adopted a cat that might try to eat Abigail's canary, and Lucas accompanied them. The cat was presently enjoying a patch of sun in the taproom, strewn across a table as though she were a large and impressive floral centerpiece.

Alma was mostly dark fur, and when they'd come across her on the road in the early morning, she'd been so filthy she looked murky brown. It wasn't until Alastair had taken his life into his own hands to bathe her, once they'd returned home and could secure a basin, that they discovered she was panther black. He had the scratches along his forearms to show the struggle, but neither of them blamed her. Most felines couldn't stand water, though Paul had read of larger ones who purportedly enjoyed it.

He was glad they hadn't found her on the way back to Trunch. They would have had a hell of a time convincing their host, a taciturn landlady in the village pub called The

Crown, to allow both a cat and Alastair to stay under her roof. As it was, she was barely ready to let any of them stay the night, coming as they did in the late evening with both Alastair and Lucas covered in dust, smelling of damp earth.

She seemed to trust Paul somewhat, even showing a bit of recognition when he'd mentioned The Queen Anne. That association seemed to shift her reticence enough to give them two rooms.

He'd said later, with an air of satisfaction and his fingers playing idly with Alastair's hair as they were curled up in bed, that landlords talked. She might've known his parents. She wasn't generous enough, however, to give anybody the means to wash as much as their faces that late in the evening and just past trading hours.

So Alastair wasn't anywhere near clean, but it didn't matter since Paul was happy to have him back above the ground. They just slept on top of the covers, using each other's warmth to keep the nighttime chill away.

Alma had trundled onto the path the next morning, after they'd set off on foot for Cromer. How she'd survived outdoors was a small mystery, as there were creatures who'd gladly attack or eat a cat, and she did behave like a pet rather than a proper stray animal. Paul thought she might have slipped out of someone's house or cottage.

Lucas didn't seem bothered at all, even slowing to pet her a little, but it seemed Torquil had a minor fear of cats. When Alastair called to her, Torquil had flinched, but merely hung back. Paul hadn't expected her to follow them. She had, and now the pub was home to a second pet. One who liked to lounge about the taproom and had already caught a mouse in the space of a night.

Less straightforward than the cat's arrival was why Lucas still walked among them, not that Paul had any particular lust for blood. But he wished to know why or if an accord had been reached. It did render things less complicated in some respects. Without a murder, Torquil hadn't become any kind of potential risk to be dealt with. Then, the reason why Lucas was still present became more apparent as they walked, and Paul listened to the conversation between him and Alastair.

They weren't trying to exclude him or rather, neither was trying to evade him.

Some of it, Paul already knew thanks to Torquil, who had kept peppering him with looks that might have translated to, *You see?*

"You were ultimately put up to this by *Bertie,*" said Alastair, bemusement and light disgust in his voice, though both emotions were very audible to Paul, "because he's *in love* with me and he thinks I slighted him." It wasn't a question, nor was it a wholehearted statement.

"I reckon he wanted to fuck with me, too," said Lucas, sounding dour. "He's different than he was. He used to be kind of smug and vapid, right? Now he's... bitter. Sharper. I can't explain it." He laughed without any humor. "He's more like us."

More like you, Paul had thought. He didn't think Alastair had a drop of bitterness in his body. He had no real cynicism or resentment, anyway.

"How the hell did you even meet? I've wanted to know for ages."

"You never asked. I delivered something to his parents' house in New Town."

"That's all?"

"How else would we meet? I brought them some meat they had ordered from Old Ross." Lucas paused. "He was hanging around the servants' door. I don't know why. But he told me he liked my shoes, and they were new, the first new ones I'd ever had..."

Alastair did not press him. "And it all went from there, hm?"

"Aye," Lucas said. "He was sweet, then, when we were boys. In his way." Paul did not think he was trying to hear it, but it almost sounded like Lucas was wistful.

At length, Alastair said to Lucas, as they had walked back home, "I never imagined he was nursing purer feelings for me, though. Not even when he kept asking me to bed. Don't have to love the man in your bed."

"It was clear he wanted you. But he never said he loved you until I saw him last." How Lucas felt about this wasn't distinct; Paul might settle on possessive.

"I reckon he might not have told anybody, even if he did," said Alastair, mystification in his voice. He shook his head slightly and the brim of his hat wavered a little. "I thought I was more of a pet to him."

This roused no small measure of indignation. Paul exclaimed, "You thought you were *what* to him? How did he treat you?" He didn't even mind Lucas' backwards glance of mild amusement at the interjection, he was so furious.

But Alastair usually couldn't be interrupted mid-thought. He simply continued past it, which was a trait Paul had learned to expect and momentarily forgotten in his pique.

Rather than answer the question, Alastair said, "I *sometimes* wondered if he might want more. Or if he felt more. But I don't think folk like him are usually prone to following their hearts when it comes to—" Then he seemed to recall Lucas and Torquil weren't the only ones there, and he favored Paul with a bright, but apologetic, smile over his shoulder.

"Don't stop on my account," said Paul, who was still as interested as could be in learning more about Alastair's past, especially if someone who was so fixated on him now knew were they both resided.

"Never, and Albert Calder is no competition to you," said Alastair, and he winked, which was always liable to make Paul a bit weak in the knees. "Even his name is ridiculous. Calling him Bert made him a little more likeable."

Lucas gave a quiet chuckle.

Paul had the sense the wink was meant to be rather distracting, and it was, but he couldn't be distracted forever. Whoever this Bert was, he'd had enough nerve to drag another person into a rather infantile, fairly dangerous, very drawn-out game just to make a point.

What Paul largely thought about on the walk back to Cromer was precisely *what* that point could be. He actually didn't mind all the walking, though it took a few hours, taking into account their stop to eat, Alma trailing after Alastair all the while.

Even now, during the morning after their return, he still pondered what Bert had been after or trying to demonstrate. Alastair hadn't offered an opinion. But this seemed to be more a matter of embarrassment, perhaps due to having slept with Bert, than the cageyness Paul used to find when asking him to bare more of his past.

Paul was angry, and he was sure Alastair would arrive at angry. But at present, he seemed more perplexed.

"You look cross," said Benson, cutting into his thoughts as

he so often did, and crossing his path to go to the kitchen, which he sometimes drifted in and out of because nobody minded. Ultimately, he hadn't needed to tend The Queen Anne for so very long and he'd let no rooms.

No one had needed one, according to Molly, which was a small blessing. Paul had not quite known how strangers would react to Benson, though he did trust him.

Benson had said, too, that Miss Garland had come to keep him company, and Paul knew she would have had things well in hand, if necessary. She was still here, evidently helping to bake a large cake in the kitchen, though Paul knew better than to be underfoot when anyone was baking. He had no gift for it and was partially convinced he ruined any cake he came near while it was in process.

"I'm not cross," said Paul, "I'm just thinking."

"Don't do too much of that." Benson slipped into the corridor, then presumably to the kitchen, and returned with a cup of tea that was actually just tea. Paul couldn't smell the alcohol he usually could from some distance away.

"Are you keeping that room, then?" Paul wanted to ask because he enjoyed Benson's company, but he didn't wish to make him feel pandered to. He just wanted to help as best he could. The best way he had was offering Benson a place where he felt safer, and freer from ghosts' intrusions, though Paul couldn't promise freedom from witchery.

"Yes, if that's all right with you, landlord."

"More than," said Paul.

"Well, that's the lads back on their way to Edinburgh," said Alastair, bustling into the taproom with his coat over his arm. "Thank fuck. That ended so much better than it could have and yet I'm not sorry to see the back of them."

Curiously, Paul said, "And you trust Lucas not to get brought in by more scheming if he sees Bert again?" Lucas' ire at having been tricked was clear enough, but Paul didn't necessarily believe it would hold. And if Bert had enough money, nearly anyone could be bought for the right price.

"Sounds like you had quite the time in Trunch," said Benson, who hadn't learned of any of their escapades yet, short of they had brought back a cat with sharp claws.

"Angel, I don't know what the hell Bert could do," said Alastair. "He's already done the most outlandish thing."

Paul was less sure, so he said what he'd thought a moment before. "He seems wealthy, and anyone can be bought."

Careless of Benson being there, not that he ever minded, Alastair strode to Paul, who stood near the bar, and brought a cool, loving palm to his cheek, then settled both palms gently on his shoulders. "Don't worry. *If* he wants to see me, I'll see him and explain—"

"He doesn't seem that interested in an explanation," Paul said, not about to be lulled by a sweet touch and calm words. "And Lucas, well, I suppose he's a little better, but I don't have to trust him."

"Lucas is abrasive and a bit overeager, mostly."

"Why didn't you kill him?"

"Oh, my," said Benson, dull with feigned shock. Paul barely smiled.

"I felt sorry for him as soon as he realized he'd been manipulated, too." Alastair's eyes were catching the light, refracting it into darkly brewed tea, which proved more distracting than his palms. "I'm not saying you ever have to accept the fact that he pointed a loaded gun at you, or that he used you as leverage. I won't. I'm far more angry about that than with him pointing a gun at me. But I don't think he was in this for blood. More a foolish lust for money and an *enormously* petty need to see me at my wit's end."

With reluctance, and after a sigh, Paul said, "I like that you're not littering the countryside with bodies, but I also liked that you were protective of me."

"That won't change. But we should practice boxing in case you need to hit someone, one day. You're a bit of a runt."

IT WAS WELL after anyone would have needed to access the back door they used for deliveries and various chores around the kitchen, so Alastair didn't quite know why he went out of his way to check if it was latched. Usually, he made use of the main door, saying good morning or good evening depending on the time he walked, if he saw anyone about.

The setting sun was glorious and burnished the steely sea with fire, so he returned from a short ramble in good spirits. He didn't need to take any exercise after walking hours yesterday. He liked walking, however, and he loved being near the water, so he went to it and came back to The Queen Anne feeling refreshed. He couldn't say he enjoyed being cold, but the chill was more bracing than demoralizing. It also seemed to have a paralyzing effect on his thoughts, which was welcome at the moment. His head was a mire of past and present, choices he had made and things that had happened to him.

He wondered if he had been too flippant with a man who

thought more of him than he would have expected, but that couldn't have been right; Bert had never voiced his expectations transparently. That said, neither had he been prone to treating Alastair with any violence. Some might laugh at such a suggestion if they saw Alastair's stature in comparison. But there were more types of violence than physical. Besides that, anyone could be subject to physically rough treatment under the right conditions.

Bert had been supercilious and rather frivolous, in Alastair's opinion. That could even veer a little into callousness, but Alastair had attributed it to his upbringing. He hadn't been taught to live with other people, much less to care about their perspectives. That itself was somewhat rare, anyway. He didn't expect anyone who'd been reared with the expectation they were within the top of their society to possess much empathy.

Even considering this, when he let himself float back to a time he didn't particularly like remembering—it had been shortly after Evie died and he was trying to be a decent father, for all he wanted to run and hide from the responsibility—Bert had shown signs of avarice and envy. Had it been due to love?

As he neared the back of The Queen Anne, bordered on either side by other establishments, one presently changing hands and the other a shop full of curiosities like old maps and antique books, he noted something hanging on the pub's door that he couldn't quite make out.

When he grew close enough to see what it was, he uttered, low in his throat, "Shit."

A stark, wretched, little mass of glossy, black feathers with a bit of blue about the top swayed gently from the back door. It seemed Lucas hadn't lied at all when he had said he'd grown out of this macabre way of sending a message. He could not have sent it now.

16

———

"Please tell me you washed your hands—we shouldn't have a protocol for dead birds here, but we do. Apparently," said Paul. He was mostly in jest, but the joke was not as farfetched as it should have been.

"Bit late to care after we've done all this, isn't it?"

"Well..." Paul chuckled, which was very intimate given how interlocked they were. "I suppose so, yes."

"Don't start me laughing," said Alastair, grinning from where he was pinned under Paul. They were tangled on the sofa that could barely hold all of Alastair, both completely naked, all their clothes strewn about the parlor.

If his parents ever looked in on him from the beyond, whatever heaven looked like for them, he dearly hoped they weren't looking now. Many happy hours had been spent here over the years, so he supposed he was just adding to them. But all the same, there were some things Mother and Father didn't need to know he was up to in their family home.

When Alastair had come to find him after discovering *another* dead corvid, he'd looked so unnerved, unsettled, that the only thing Paul could think to do was this. No doubt there were a number of more rational things one could do, like talk about it or offer to help Alastair dispose of the pitiable thing.

Anyway, he already had done so. But the crow bore an ominous note this time, and he'd saved it. It wasn't even a sentence, merely *All my love, AC x* written neatly in black ink on a bit of blue-tinged paper that had a more expensive hand-feel than any paper Paul had in his possession.

The handwriting was Bert's, said Alastair, but he quickly assured Paul they hadn't exchanged any notes past short and pragmatic ones. In other words, Bert did not have heaps of love letters at his disposal, which did make Paul feel better.

That little scrap of paper was somewhere with their clothes, either on the floor or set on a piece of furniture, perhaps the dainty circular table opposite the sofa. He couldn't remember where Alastair had left it. The last hour was all rather a blur, and now he felt both better and worse.

Worse, because they knew who had sent the first crow and it meant Bert had probably been watching them intermittently for at least a week, maybe even a fortnight, depending on how long he had been in Cromer before Lucas and Torquil. He could not have been staying at The Red Lion, same as them, or he likely would have been noticed.

The idea of him being here and undetected turned Paul's stomach. "It's good to laugh," he said, "or fuck—rather than worry."

"Are you so worried?"

"Killing birds and leaving them for people to find isn't an indication of someone being in their right mind, so yes, I am." He kissed Alastair's cheek, then added, "I can't have this conversation while I'm inside you."

"Fair enough," said Alastair, and he shifted slightly so Paul could rearrange himself. Though it was a little messy for both of them, and he wondered if the sofa might need to be cleaned after all this, Paul settled atop Alastair in a less entwined manner. He didn't mind the mess when it was theirs; in previous arrangements, he had been much more fastidious than this, sometimes to the chagrin of his partners who perceived his dislike as snobbishness. It wasn't, really.

He just saw it as vulnerable and more intimate than he wished to be with most people. Alastair wasn't most people.

Sighing as Alastair's hands roved his back and then petted his neck, Paul said, "Now that's two crows, as well as a whole trip to a… I don't know what to call that derelict farmhouse. It's not really a landing point, because it's not on the beach."

"I think it might have been a lookout, of a sort," Alastair murmured. He would know. "Years ago. All that room for clandestine storage, a good vantage point when the trees were younger or better kept, maybe even false floors or walls inside." He even ventured to tease, "We should go back and explore. Perhaps turn it into another public house or hostelry."

"No," said Paul immediately, albeit pleasantly.

Alastair did laugh at how quickly he said it. "All right."

"My point, I think, is this former lover of yours seems unwell."

Graceful fingertips stroked into his hair, playing with it as Alastair seemed to think before he spoke. "He did always have an edge of being unloved. I don't know how else to put it. He was greedy for warm regard. We weren't together, to my mind, so much as we had an accord."

"Apparently, he felt differently."

"Oh, now I've no doubt that he did," said Alastair. "Not if he's gone to all of this trouble. But what I mean is, perhaps his rot goes deeper than that greed. Maybe things have happened to him in these past years to make his brain go funny."

"Maybe it's inbreeding."

"He isn't *so* high in society that I think that would be a problem," Alastair replied, but Paul could tell he was tickled.

"What are we going to do? I'm not waiting for a whole... murder of murdered crows. And it's supposed to be terrible luck to kill seabirds, so I don't want him getting bored and moving on to them."

"Well, I can start by finding out where he's staying, then I can go talk to him. He had a country house in Norfolk"—Paul wondered with a quick burn of spite if Alastair had visited it —"but I wouldn't have any idea exactly where it is." The envy flickered away. "It's certainly not Cromer Hall. I seem to recall Overstrand being mentioned, but I never listened very closely to him."

Nearly laughing, for this was said with an amount of dismissal that would presumably set someone like Bert to fury, Paul said, "I wonder if you should have, and then he wouldn't have been such an instigator." Paul did not think he should ever meet Bert. In truth, it could not end well in any sense of the word, for he would try his best to assert himself and who knew where that would lead. Wealth did not intimidate him, and neither did so-called good breeding or respectability.

Arching up, Alastair kissed Paul gently, and their lips met

carefully before melding with more urgency. "Don't borrow trouble. I can *feel* your mind spinning like a top."

The kissing almost worked its magic to coax Paul into feeling more serene, or at least aroused again. But he said, still concerned that one man had managed to induce this much chaos and still lingered quite near, likely to create more, "I can't help but think you may be underestimating him. He did manage to arrange quite a bit of upheaval these last few days."

He even wondered if Bert was linked to his vision of sinking through cold, dark water, wrists and ankles bound. He might think it was extreme to assume this of a stranger— if they hadn't just been embroiled in such a dubious adventure.

Or if there hadn't been two birds stuck to the door.

But that premonition hadn't come to pass, while the tense exchange between Alastair and Lucas had. He had not been there underground, but some version of it must have, judging by how their journey home had transpired. And although Paul couldn't corroborate if James and Arthur really had the conversation he'd seen, he reckoned it had happened or soon would. Futures, after all, weren't always far ahead.

"Lucas caused it, too."

"We know that Bert is nearby, though," said Paul. He hoped his sense of danger was just more easily activated than Alastair's because he hadn't been part of the demimonde as a youngster. Perhaps Alastair was more immune to the prospect of hazards than he was. He knew more now about him than he had, but there were clearly still things to unearth; they might account for Alastair's outward equanimity when it came to danger. "Was he always drawn to—sorry—criminals?"

Torquil had said, as had Lucas, that Bert was interested in Alastair specifically. Rather, that he was mad for him. Paul could empathize with that madness, but instinct told him Bert was the sort of man who also viewed others' experiences and lives as things to be romanticized. As though poverty and the like were things to be observed and consumed for entertainment, not allayed.

Meanwhile Alastair, Paul reckoned, had been so starved for affection and companionship that he just accepted being fetishized or studied to have a physical association with Bert. If Alastair was as bad at communicating then as he was now, it was little wonder that Bert had made assumptions about the depth of his regard. That, paired with any amount of either arrogance or simply being used to getting what one wanted, might mean Bert truly convinced himself he was in love with Alastair and that Alastair loved him in return.

It wasn't how Paul approached anything. But this type of possessiveness, or investment, or whatever it was on Bert's part, had to underlie what they'd just gone through.

It made him uneasy, for desperate men could prove dangerous. His family trade had taught him as much, with spurned or recently unemployed men proving the most capricious while intoxicated. He felt it was equally true when they were sober; they were often just better at concealing it.

Like Alastair, he shared the concern that Bert had been watching them at least intermittently since the first poor crow. Before then, in truth. He had wondered what motivation could underpin such a rancorous thing. The answer was, plainly, rejection or loss.

Perhaps the willingness to wait to exact revenge was one thing Bert and Lucas had in common all along. They must have had more in common than that alone.

He felt Alastair's smile against his lips, followed by a quick nip of teeth to the lower one. He moaned, just a bit, thinking of what often followed the gesture. Still, he waited for a proper reply.

"Yes, he did seem to fancy himself as one of us. Really, he just showed up one day with Lucas, who let him tag along. They were childhood mates, you see. You heard him—at first, he delivered meat to the Calders."

He did not quite see. "Did Lucas teach him to kill birds and leave them hanging around?"

Instead of feeling a smile, he felt a frown. "He must have. I doubt he would have picked it up from one of his Cambridge friends."

"I wouldn't put it past a few of them, either, but you did say Lucas had done it." Misery and cruelty could wear genteel masks, Paul knew, and the gentility might well allow for them to go undetected. In this case, however, it seemed most logical to assume Bert had picked up at least some of his more alarming behaviors from his boyhood friend.

"God, that is true," said Alastair. "I would bet Cambridge shields all manner of secret societies and the like." He kissed Paul lightly, who didn't care to speculate on any potential dark doings at Cambridge.

"Then, at some point, you two became lovers."

The response came on a sigh. "He wore me down; I was lonely. It was just whenever he visited. He had a house, but he didn't live there all the time. I think it must have been his brother's, actually." Though it was completely outside of

Paul's experience, he knew moneyed families kept houses where it suited them. "I never went there."

He never invited you there, you mean.

And *lonely* in this case probably meant something more like *aroused.* Paul wouldn't say that directly, for he didn't see anything wrong with it. He was simply jealous, and he knew it. "He eased your loneliness."

"I was alone—Evie was gone. Not that we ever slept together."

"I wouldn't have expected you to be alone forever. But maybe you could have been more discerning? He sounds…" Paul said, after a few words almost crossed his tongue, "tiresome."

Alastair arched under him, slipping a hand between them, and Paul nearly thrummed with anticipation. With one hand still wound in Paul's hair and the other grazing his stomach, on its way lower, Alastair said, "He is. Was. But I'm incredibly discerning now."

17

A few days after Lucas and Torquil had gone and a second crow had been thrown into the sea, Alastair decided to send another mysterious letter. He wanted to reason with Bert himself and in person, make it clear that he was not welcome and neither was his meddling. This letter, Paul did not even glimpse. In retrospect, Alastair realized he should have taken greater care to hide his letters to James. But perhaps part of him had yearned to be found out.

He didn't know where Bert was staying, though he had to be somewhere near, and he undoubtedly still kept some kind of watch on The Queen Anne. The thought made his skin crawl.

Once evening fell, then night, Alastair waited until everyone had bedded down and the building echoed with naught but old wood creaking and the periodic muffled snore. As Halloween drew ever nearer, he couldn't help but feel unsettled by noises that were otherwise his new ordinary and he almost expected to sight a ghost. Evie, perhaps, or

Paul's mother or father or grandfather tending to the taproom. But it was nothing save the temperature exacting its power over an old wooden structure, and someone with what sounded like a formidable head cold.

When he was certain all were asleep, he slipped out of bed and left a discreetly folded note on the back door. He had scrawled, *Meet near the west side of the church?*

It was, Alastair had decided, the mildest he could be.

Though it had taken a bit of time for him to recognize his emotions, he had arrived at angry and felt threatened by this new complication. Brevity was best, else he would devolve into obscenities. Mother had not insisted he be reasonably educated just so he could leave letters strewn with blasphemies and expletives, but it was sorely tempting to devolve into bile.

The church was clear enough. He reckoned many a mariner had seen St Peter and St Paul's from the sea, although the structure itself was in a poor state. Benson remarked that some rich man had begun some kind of restoration, but it seemed those proceedings had stopped or slowed. All the flint and woeful dilapidation would provide a suitably atmospheric place for a covert discussion, during which he wished to say these games must end.

The next morning, the note was gone, as he expected it would be. When night fell—long after it fell, for he did not want to accidentally wake anyone and have to explain what he was doing—he crept downstairs and opened the back door to his note's reply.

Of course, darling—tomorrow would be ideal; perhaps at 3 in the morning? it read. *Even your landlord should be well asleep by then.*

Alastair threw it into the mostly dead fire in the taproom, poking the sleeping embers under the narrow shred of paper until they consumed it. Then, because he was no barbarian, he banked the fire again. He could have done without the endearment, more still without the observation about his landlord. He carried disgruntled sentiment all the way to the last five minutes before he was to see Bert, when it bled into resentful ire.

He'd wanted to speak to Bert well away from Paul, in the hopes that the entire affair could be concluded without further strife for him. He had been remarkably tolerant of circumstances that might have driven other men to fury, but Alastair could tell he was trying to make sense of it all.

Bert's scent reached him as he waited near the still rather bedraggled church. It was some heady, probably au courant, perfume that made his nose itch. In truth, it likely had the power to drive off any ghosts of medieval people who might have been buried somewhere under his own boots.

After a few moments, Bert came into view, looking no less immaculately dressed than the last time they'd seen each other.

It had not been as long as Alastair thought; perhaps a year and a half ago. His sense of time passing had never been as precise as other people's, or so he'd been told derisively by his father and teasingly by his friends. But the last time he'd met with Bert, it had been several months before he'd left Edinburgh and installed his son as the man of their house. There had been a quick, careless afternoon before that departure, and he'd said nothing of his ambiguous, but urgent, plans. It meant little to him emotionally, no more than eating half a sandwich and drinking warm tea might.

With a clear, crisp night sky, he could see Bert's face well enough, and anyway, Bert came too close for comfort. Alastair took a step back, and the little smile on his foxlike face went into more of an unkind smirk.

"My boy," said Bert, keeping his voice down, presumably for the sake of the hour, "it is so good to see you."

"Think you've been seeing rather a lot of me." A more intelligent thing might have been to forgo pointing this out, but Alastair was too overwhelmed to lean on intelligence.

"Oh, you should know it's actually quite difficult to see anything *inside* that ramshackle public house." This was delivered with the tenor of a quip.

He narrowed his eyes, almost more offended at the description of his home than he was at the confirmation of Bert having had an eye on it. "Somehow, I don't consider that much comfort." He would not contemplate whether Bert had also heard anything; Paul preferred to keep his windows open for as long as he could before any chill set in, and so far, autumn had proven fickle, warm one day and cool the next.

"I know how much you like your privacy," said Bert.

Privacy and separation had been at the center of his terms for their relationship, such as it was; he had never wished to live with Bert, for example, nor had he ever asked Bert to remain loyal to him alone. They were free to live as they each needed or preferred to, and Alastair had been under the assumption that Bert was content with something more casual. That, of course, had been wrong, as recent events demonstrated.

The main thing he remained unsure of was duration—had Bert always wanted this, or was it a newer desire wrought by nostalgia and romanticism?

Then, the thought instigated by nothing except the glitter of a gold signet ring on Bert's left pinky, Alastair wondered how a man with such soft hands had managed to kill two birds. If he'd dressed in uglier clothes than this when he'd done it. If indeed he had done it himself and not simply told someone else to do it.

Mere moments in his presence were enough to show that something about Bert had shifted and given way to a more unstable quality.

Where he'd once been superciliously brittle and sometimes endearingly naïve, his little gestures and demeanor had gone sharp. Lucas had been right to say he'd changed. Alastair believed he *had* killed the birds, though it would have been somewhat comforting to think otherwise.

To what end, Alastair did not care to find out. For once, his natural curiosity did not win over an urgent need to make certain his life would remain as it had been over this last year. He sighed. "What is it that you want?"

The answer was brutal in its directness. "You." Bert took another pace toward him, and Alastair might have sprinted from the eagerness in his expression.

Still, he held his ground. "You can't have me."

"I can give you a better life than this."

"No, you can't."

"I have everything my family has to offer," said Bert, as though he had not heard, "all of it. Comfort. Stability. Money, the houses. There *are* only three and they're each rather small, but one is right here, right near the—"

"I don't need money. Or a house."

Bert's fervor was starting to unsettle Alastair, enough that he could not laugh at the thought of *only* three houses when some men had none. It also wouldn't make much of a difference, he felt, to try arguing that his own feelings did not match Bert's. He took a deep breath and kept meeting Bert's eyes, though it was difficult for him to maintain. Hard to see much color in the cloudless but deep night, and their blue was desaturated gray.

"Of course you don't. Lucas told me about how clever you'd been with that Adair girl, how her father was incredibly generous upon her safe return—"

"Then why did you offer me money?" said Alastair, allowing some annoyance to seep into his voice. "If you know so much, why start with that?"

Like a horse troubled by a fly, Bert shook his head. "I did always wonder how you seemed so well off for a man of your particular origin." The words' gentility didn't fool Alastair; Bert's incredulity had always been evident to him, even if he had been woeful at seeing other things, like the magnitude of his regard. It had to be possessiveness more than love. "How you could afford that charwoman who—"

"Morwenna," Alastair interjected. "Her name is Morwenna."

"Morwenna," repeated Bert, though his lack of care for the detail of her name was writ in the dismissive wave of his right hand. "How your house was reasonably fine, not shabby at all. I came to call one day, months back, and she answered the door with a scowl."

"She can't speak. Well, she doesn't speak. I don't know if she absolutely cannot."

"She wrote," Bert said, "after she let me in." Alastair inferred this meant only that Bert had badgered Morwenna until she brought him into the small parlor and written what he wanted to know. He might have paid her a bit, too. Even if the man could murder crows or orchestrate a fool's errand from Edinburgh to the Norfolk coast, it still felt unlikely he could be rough with a person. "And I learned you'd left indefinitely, though she didn't have a proper address for you."

Indefinite was a generous thing for Morwenna to assume. Although, if it appeared to her that James was now simply managing the household finances, she likely believed Alastair would be coming back. It wasn't unheard of for a young man of James's age to assume such responsibilities in his father's absence, however long that might be.

"I had to go," said Alastair. His words were tight and quiet.

He recalled Paul's way of putting it. That had been the instant when he finally knew what had driven him so abruptly to leave. He had thought it was a permutation of his own restlessness, perhaps his love for excitement and adventure, but it was more self-preservation than wanderlust alone.

A nightbird called from an overgrown tree somewhere behind Bert, interrupting the faint rhythm of the sea. After a pause, Bert said, "I understand *that* far better now I'm expected to undertake all sorts of responsibilities to access an inheritance that, quite frankly, was probably never intended to be mine."

Uncertain if this was a genuine attempt on his part to empathize and connect, for they had not even started to discuss Trunch and Lucas and anything that had transpired of late, Alastair said, "Responsibilities?" Trusting did not come easily to him, and trust was not about to feel more natural if it were directed toward Bert. He was rapidly losing sight of his goals in this conversation.

With a sigh that might have been earnest, Bert said, "Marriage, fathering a child—an heir, as it were—all that sort of thing. I *am* trying to find ways around it, legally speaking." He gave a forced little chuckle. "It's so very old fashioned."

This did strike Alastair heavily. He could not quite feel sympathy for a rich man being unable to access yet more money, but he did know what a toll it took to appear unbothered by certain expectations and assumptions. His own father, after all, seemed to take macabre pleasure in his marriage to a woman.

The other Calders had likely known of Bert's persuasion. As his older brother would have been the one leaving behind this most recent will, it seemed there was little allyship between siblings. Bert didn't seem upset by his brother's death, merely a bit perplexed that he stood to gain all that had been left behind. He must not be an uncle, for his nephew would have been next in that case.

Quite a different situation from what Paul described about his own childhood. The Apollyons sounded almost gloriously accepting, his seer's abilities posing more of a potential problem than who he slept with. He had still inherited a whole pub and nobody, including his younger brother who had married and now had a child, stopped it or made it contingent upon specific criteria.

Alastair would not want to be Bert. He did not envy him his resources, all of which were dependent upon a façade and traditions. "Very."

"But if," said Bert, "it comes down to me marrying some girl, I suppose I can do that. I have other things to occupy my time, really, and if you would—"

"No."

"You don't even know what it is I'm going to say, my boy."

"I'm not your boy," said Alastair, "and nothing you can say will persuade me to, what? Be your mistress?"

"Well, I wouldn't put it so crudely as that, but if you must."

"I'm already somebody's wife."

"Plenty of wives are also mistresses," said Bert. His voice was light, but his eyes were hawkish.

"I didn't send that note to talk about anything like this," said Alastair. The nightbird called again, sounding alone and desolate, if such a creature could be. No other bird had yet returned its call. "What the hell were you thinking, sending Lucas down here for old loot you *knew* didn't exist?" How, he couldn't say. But Bert had known. "Leaving crows on the door?" He bore down on Bert, putting both hands on his shoulders and then clutching his lapels hard.

"We need to be together," said Bert, almost serenely, the physical contact seemingly doing the opposite of what Alastair wanted it to do.

"No, *you* want me," Alastair said, "and that's not the same thing. Besides, I'm not the man you knew."

"Have you changed so much, then?"

Thinking back to their final and rushed encounter, Alastair wanted to insist the answer to the question was yes. He wasn't sure Bert would believe him. "You didn't really answer me."

Bert reached up and gently disengaged his hands, but only because Alastair let him do so. Then he brushed off his shoulders and righted his lapels. "I've been frightfully bored of late, bored and frustrated. When I saw Lucas in that dirty pub and we started to talk like it was old times, I wondered if it was fate."

So many things crossed Alastair's mind, strayed nearly to his lips, and didn't linger long enough for him to ask. An uncanny sheen was in Bert's eyes, covetous and intent, and it proved too distracting. The story that had induced Lucas to come to Cromer felt least important, but it became Alastair's foremost thought. "His source had family knowledge."

Bert gave a satisfied little sigh. "Oh, yes."

Unconvinced, Alastair said, "*You* had family who were smugglers."

"Every family has a black sheep, as it were."

Deciding not to push the logic too much, for he could see Bert wanted him to ask far more about his free-trading family and Alastair would not give him the benefit of enquiring too deeply, he asked, "Did the farmhouse belong to your people, then?"

"If you want to have a proper conversation with me, I won't be doing it out here in the dead of night."

"I'm afraid I don't know if I'm capable of a proper conversation with you," said Alastair. "But I think you should leave Cromer."

"*I'm* afraid that is not an option," Bert said.

"Why the hell not?"

"I live nearby, now. Which I wanted to say before you interjected." After a pause, Bert added, "I can see it upsets you. If it is any comfort, as I said, there *are* the three homes. I may not be in residence all of the time."

Although Bert said he could see the way he had caused upset, Alastair doubted he meant to apologize for causing it.

The need to howl at him, demand why this of all things was so important that he had to interpose himself into Alastair's life, was urgent, immense. It couldn't be love that drove him.

Alastair knew what love was, now, and it wasn't whatever unctuous, acquisitive thing he felt seeping from Bert. Even if it was, and this was just how he experienced love, Alastair wanted no part of it. He wondered what had happened to render possessiveness, perhaps insecurity, into such predatory tenacity.

Yet he could guess this new quality wasn't about to evaporate. It hadn't failed Bert when he drew Lucas into such a game, and Alastair understood it wouldn't fail him now. Knowing this—acknowledging he couldn't come up against it and win for the moment—he did something he was not used to doing.

He gave up.

"Fine," he murmured. "If you're so local, there's no need to keep killing things. Ordinary notes will do, or just come to The Queen Anne."

At that, Bert grinned. "How perfectly lovely."

But in giving up, he merely created space for receiving answers to his questions, as well as determining his next move.

EPILOGUE

We need to fall, and we need to be aware of it; for if we did not fall, we should not know how weak and wretched we are of ourselves, nor should we know our Maker's marvelous love so fully...

— MOTHER JULIAN OF NORWICH

"Paul."

He woke to the whisper of his name with a scowl. "What?" But he realized there was a soft, warm hand on his shoulder, and the gesture's weight helped him catalogue the whisper. His scowl melted into a smile. "I assume we're not on fire or you'd be less calm."

"We're not on fire," Alastair said, and when Paul opened his eyes, he could just make out that Alastair was fully dressed, his single-breasted overcoat buttoned and hanging properly on his body. "I'm just trying not to be as covert as I have been."

On a yawn, Paul asked, "Did you have to start that

admirable endeavor by waking me from a dead sleep?" As soon as he asked himself how he could see so well in the middle of the night, he registered a candle's glow that likely came from one of their mismatched bedside tables.

"Perhaps not, but it's not so far from when you wake."

"No?" Frowning, he drew himself into a sitting position against the pillows and looked balefully at Alastair, whose hair was mussed as though it had been ruffled by a strong breeze. "Where have you been?"

"The church."

"Church?"

"Yes. And I was thinking, again, about how you really should pay Muriel a visit."

Any warmth he felt upon registering the presence of his lover, the calm security of his presence, was dissipating; something was deeply amiss. "Have you been drinking?"

"Not a bit."

"What the hell is wrong?"

"Bert *lives nearby* now."

Of all the mad things he expected, he hadn't anticipated it, and for such a simple concept, it roused an uncommon amount of dread. Alastair sat by his side atop the counterpane, appearing for all the world as apprehensive as Paul felt. It was not usual for his expression to be so forlorn, and so Paul rallied to assure him they could manage this development. "Did you go to see him?"

One short nod was all he received.

"How suitably gothic, that it was next to a church." It was marginally less uncomfortable to imagine the two meeting there instead of Bert's country house, which must be removed enough from Cromer to merit some small journey. Still, little could be done to assuage his nerves overall, and he did not wish to examine how he felt now knowing Bert had been skulking about. Not only to leave menacing notes or corvid corpses, but plainly to watch the object of his affections.

"I didn't want to go anywhere that was his, and I didn't want to have him here while you were asleep. Neutral ground was preferable."

He did not know if he wanted Bert in his public house even when he was awake; the thought of seeing the architect of their recent and dubious adventures was rather too much. Nonetheless, he appreciated the sentiment. How Alastair felt was legible to Paul, almost more so than his own emotions, for he looked smaller than Paul had ever seen him, drawn in upon himself as though ashamed it had all come to this.

"I'm not going to see Muriel," he said gently. He swallowed and watched the candlelight shift on the wall to paint the old wardrobe in the corner with warmth. "I'm not leaving you."

This, of all he could have said, was apparently what Alastair most needed to hear. He neither argued nor dissembled, and instead leaned forward to grasp Paul's hand like a rope cast to a man overboard at sea. A quiet, potent *thank you* left his lips, as though it were the same overboard man's prayer gone from water to sky.

AN HOUR after Alastair had left him by the church, Bert still lingered. He was lost in his own thoughts, almost elated at what was bound to come to pass. Alastair, the force of energy that he was, would decide to be with him. He was sure of it.

The only thing he was not sure of was precisely how or when, and the road to a life together had indeed proved rather treacherous. He should have remembered that, even though he had premonitions, they presented their own timings. For him, and he did not know another soul who could do what he did, the *when* was trickier than the *what* or *if.*

He had seen Alastair telling him yes, saying so without reservation, and in his premonition, he looked much as he did now. Still, the future was a delicate business. This was in evidence given his recent visit to Alastair's house, which he no longer lived in but had left for that son of his. He went without word or warning. Despite all of this, Bert was confident their futures were one and the same; he had even seen Alastair within much plusher and higher circumstances than outside a crumbling church.

To be precise, he'd seen him within the country house near Cromer which he now owned. Bert knew if things were supposed to happen, and it had not been the case yet that something he'd seen had not occurred.

But like other personal matters in his life, he inferred quite early that he was not meant to talk about what he saw or even to actively encourage it by giving into flights of fancy. Some of this circumspectness was learned, and some of it was established by his parents, who disparaged any softness and caprice until it either departed or festered.

Mother and Father were devout; Bert himself was rational. Although they did not always agree so neatly, science and religion seemed quite adamant: he was not part of the natural order of things in more than one way. Science denied his senses and foresight, while religion denounced his desire.

The only place where he had felt tenuously normal was

amongst those of Lucas's ilk, thieves and other unfortunates of a world immortalized in fiction, poetry, and songs. Even there, he had not spoken about his mind's ability to see forward, convinced even the demimonde had no place for it. Since boyhood, he had witnessed things that were yet to happen in his dreams.

His elder brother tripping down some stairs and splitting his lip had been first; quite bewildered at the age of six, he'd still had some sense after it happened that the coincidence shouldn't be mentioned to Mother or Father. Nor should any of the others he witnessed, the kitchen fire that left Cook with burns on his forearm, the redecorating of the London townhouse's parlor from greens to purples.

Sighing as he considered the old church's flint wall, he reflected that neither of his parents had been the sort of person who was capable of much affection; he was given no indication that he should seek them out for advice or perspective. To them, he was excess stock, another son who was neither particularly welcomed nor derided.

He had some awareness early in his life that witchcraft and the like were not to be tolerated. He was never told they did not exist, after all. Father had been brought up to be that quaint variety of Christian person who, rather than perhaps find solace in the idea of an afterlife that could be navigated by human spirits, believed such things were dark temptations.

Bert could not have imagined what Father would say should he be found out, in any sense, either for loving men or seeing the future. Neither suited Father's views.

Luckily, even when he was a young boy, his parents were content to let him do as he wished so long as he did not make much of a fuss. Then, as he grew older, it became more apparent that censure would be the likely response to any honesty. Freedom was not worth the risk of losing his creature comforts, such as they were. All of what he had seen was quite mundane. He kept it to himself as he lived out his days in a way that might drive others to envy—pursuit of hobbies, assignations, delving into any walks of life Lucas had introduced him to.

Far worse, he had often thought, to tell the truth and be committed than it was to remain so silent. He would not admit that a sort of madness was the price of such quiet, a persistent sense of hunger stalking him until he went to sleep every night. Hunger for what, he could not say, yet it had followed him into adulthood. He had to conclude it was caused by never speaking about his ability or his inclination, both of which he masked as best he could.

He tried to appear as others expected him to, including when he'd spoken to Lucas about his shoes some years ago when they were boys. It was a strategy for self-preservation to seem like nothing but a wealthy younger son, someone who cared for the finer things in life but was not above kindness when it suited him. He and Lucas began a friendship, and as they grew older, there were a few times when he wondered if it might become more intimate.

But Lucas was subjected to his own type of madness, one wrought by poverty and violence, and sensuality did not come naturally to him. Bert, meanwhile, struggled with his looming hunger and the restlessness that gnawed at him.

One cold November evening, Lucas introduced Bert to Alastair Gow and the nature of Bert's visions changed, shifting from mishaps and fancies that might occur to others, to quite intoxicating glimpses of Alastair and himself in a tidy, pretty little bedroom. Most of the moments he would eventually spend there he saw, or had already seen, by the time he was living them.

Beyond that, he had not seen Alastair's departure from Edinburgh. *Perhaps fickle is a better word than delicate when it comes to the future.*

Even now, he hadn't dreamt much besides Alastair in the country house, and meeting with him in this very churchyard. He glanced around, amused that the scene was as he had expected. He hadn't heard anything—anticipatory dreams were often like that, often devoid of something quite normal like sound—but the cold, the soft wind, the look of desperation within Alastair's countenance had all been expected.

To be sure, Alastair's pretty landlord posed something of a problem now, but Bert was undaunted. He was a consummate meddler and now had more wealth at his disposal than he had ever possessed. Paul Apollyon signified little of note, and anybody whose means were slim could be tempted with the right amount of money. This young fellow, this nobody, could not love Alastair as much as Bert did. Paul did not have nearly as much to offer, either.

Besides, Bert could wait a little longer. He often found ways to amuse himself and defuse his ill feelings by interfering in others' circumstances. Lucas, for example, had not *needed* to come all this way only to embroil himself in nothing —it had felt good to goad someone who so clearly held a grudge. All it had taken was some reminiscing and half-formed, insider gossip about a free traders' drop gone wrong.

That it had actually happened so near to where Alastair

now resided was not luck, in Bert's view. It was confirmation that this was, perhaps, divinely guided meddling. He liked to see what people might do when set against each other, or when something strange happened to them.

As he sat on an old bench with a crack down the middle and watched the stars become even more obscured behind churning clouds, Bert was convinced that fortune at last favored him. Too much had fallen into place for it not to be so. Mr. Apollyon would tire of his meddling, and soon pose no obstacle at all.

ALSO BY CAMILLE DUPLESSIS

Threads of Wyrd

The Kraken and The Canary

Like Silk Breathing

The Only Story

Unfair Winds

Of Flint and Fortune

ABOUT THE AUTHOR

Camille is a thalassophile who sadly spent too long residing in Chicago, where there's just a very large lake and no sea. An enquiring and possibly over-educated mind, she's been described as "the politest contrarian." Though everyone believes she's tall, she's not. Likewise, she doesn't dress in all-black.